PROMISE OF REDEMPTION

SEARCHING HEARTS
BOOK FIVE

ELLIE ST. CLAIR

CONTENTS

Facebook: Ellie St. Clair

Cover by AJF Designs

Do you love historical romance? Receive access to a free ebook, as well as exclusive content such as giveaways, contests, freebies and advance notice of pre-orders through my mailing list!

Sign up here!

Also By Ellie St. Clair
Searching Hearts
Duke of Christmas (prequel)
Quest of Honor
Clue of Affection
Hearts of Trust
Hope of Romance
Promise of Redemption

Searching Hearts Box Set (Books 1-5)

For a full list of all of Ellie's books, please see
www.elliestclair.com/books.

PROLOGUE

"So, how is that son of yours?"

"Which one?"

"The future duke, of course."

The current Duke of Ware sighed, looking upward, hopeful that God would hear his silent prayers. "Daniel is just the same as always. Hard, angry, bitter, alone — as he has been for years now."

The Marquess of Burrton nodded sagely, his wispy gray hair bobbing as he did so. "Still keeping himself closeted away?"

Heaviness settled over the Duke's heart when he thought of his son, though he would never reveal such emotion to his friend. "I do not know what he does with his days, nor what he intends to do with his life. I have taught him all I can, of course, so he is more than ready to take on the title when the time comes, but he shows no enthusiasm for it."

"And he is not married."

"No."

"He will need an heir — and I can see that troubles you,"

Lord Burrton said, inclining his head. "I understand that. I went through the same thing with my boy."

A chuckle worked itself free as the Duke remembered how Lord Burrton had often complained about his son doing nothing but throwing money away in London. One year later, however, and the young man was now married with a child on the way. "I suppose it means that, in time, all will be well if we put our trust in our children."

Lord Burrton snorted. "As you did with your other children?"

Recalling the measures he and his wife had taken to try to push their children to find matches, the Duke shifted uncomfortably in his seat. It had all worked out wonderfully, however, with his children now not only married but happy. With one exception.

"And do not think that I waited for Henderson to make the right decision on his own, either," Lord Burrton replied, with a wide grin of self-satisfaction. "It is my own doing that brought about his married state. I threw the two of them together, I did."

Frowning, the Duke sat up a little straighter and sharpened his gaze, regarding his friend carefully. "You did?"

"Of course I did!" the marquess exclaimed, as though Ware should have known. "You did not think I would let my son continue in his foolish ways without doing something about it, did you?"

A little surprised, the Duke sat back in his chair and studied his friend. They had been companions for over two decades, and he considered Burrton to be one of his closest friends. They'd shared much of their lives with one another, although apparently, he did not know everything that Burrton had been up to lately.

"So, you found your son a bride," Ware murmured,

thoughtfully. "Did you find any difficulty in securing his agreement?"

"None whatsoever," Burrton replied, with a glint in his eye. "I simply threatened to take away a great deal of his fortune if he did not."

Ware frowned, rolling his glass between his fingers. "I do not think I could do that to Daniel. The lad has been through enough."

Lord Burrton chuckled, lifting his brandy glass with a wink for the Duke. "Of course you could. You can do whatever you need to in order to secure the future of your line. Sure, Daniel has had his trials, but it has been years now. Where is that second son of yours, anyway? He is not the kind of gentleman who could take over the line if Daniel fails to do so, I don't think."

A slight nudge of regret tugged at the Duke as he thought of Thomas, but he brushed it away quickly. The boy — the man, he should say — was happy now. Ware had pushed him to the sea, and Thomas had turned around and made a life for himself. Burrton was just being blunt and direct, as usual, although the Duke didn't think he ever *intended* to be either rude or condescending.

"My second son did well for himself in the navy," he now said, slowly, "but he has chosen his own path for a time. I know he would step up to the task if it was required of him, however."

"A free spirit, eh?" Lord Burrton grinned, waggling one finger in Ware's direction. "Always a little trickier to manage, that kind of son. However, your eldest son appears not to be that way, although I will confess that I do not quite know what to make of a gentleman who likes to remain at his remote estate and very rarely attend any kind of social gathering."

"I think that is the problem," the Duke agreed, somewhat

sadly. "I do not know much about my son either any longer. I cannot tell you why he shuns society and why he insists on remaining at his estate for the Season. He did attend before, some years ago, but has not done so for some time now."

That had always weighed rather heavily on his soul, the fact that he had lost such touch with his eldest son when they had once been so close. They had spent a great deal of time together when Daniel was growing up, in between his stints at Eton. It was important that a duke's son learn his role for when the time came for him to take his place. However, while Ware was certain that Daniel knew what was expected of him and he could put it all into practice when required — evident by the fact Daniel ran his own, smaller estate very well — a coldness had formed between them.

Ever since the death of the woman Daniel was courting, it was as if he had built a wall of ice around himself, keeping to his own home and very rarely venturing from it. At least, he did not think that Daniel often took himself away, for there was rarely news that his son had been seen in London or Bath, or any other of his once-frequent haunts.

"You are aware that I have a daughter."

Lord Burrton's voice broke into the Duke's thoughts, and he stared up at his friend in surprise while the marquess poured himself another brandy.

"She is not remarkably pretty, that I will say, but she is as accomplished as you would expect any young lady to be," Burrton continued, regarding the Duke with an almost serene expression on his face. "She is well mannered, genteel, quiet, and with a decent brain in her head." He chuckled, shrugging his shoulders. "I must say she is actually altogether *too* practical, but one cannot stop one's daughter from reading, and that is all she appears to do!"

"She does not enjoy society?"

Lord Burrton appeared to grow a little uncomfortable,

his eyes darting away as he shifted in his seat. "Truth be told, old friend, I have not encouraged her in the way I ought to have done. She has no mother, as you know, and so I put all my energies into finding my son a bride before thinking of her." He shrugged slightly, as though the death of his wife some years ago was an excuse for ignoring his daughter's future.

"I have always intended to take her to London, but I can hardly stomach the idea of having to take her about places in the hope that she will find a suitable gentleman. She has a decent dowry, of course, but I know what the gentlemen of the *ton* are like. They will not care for a bluestocking who fills her head with knowledge, regardless of how amiable she is. I always feared she would be something of a wallflower, and I did not wish that upon her." He shrugged again, looking back at the Duke. "As I said, she is not a diamond of the first water or anything close to it, but I am sure she would do. Now I myself have … prospects, and I realize it would be much easier to take a new wife if my daughter were married."

"Ah, so you are serious about Lady Aster," the Duke said, grinning at his friend, who nodded back at him with a satisfied smile. "And you are thinking that my son could marry your daughter."

Lord Burrton nodded, his eyes alight with hope. "I think that would be a marvelous idea," he said, as though Ware had come up with the plan himself. "It would save me having to fret about whom Christina is to marry, and it means that your son will finally have himself a wife and, hopefully in time, an heir."

The Duke nodded slowly, considering things carefully. The rest of his children had all married and were now happy and settled — which meant that Daniel's lack of interest in the matrimonial state was now all the more evident. Even his wife had nearly given up hope, and she was as stubborn as they came.

"It would be a good match," Lord Burrton continued, eagerly. "Joining our families together, eh? You know that I would not present her if I did not think her capable of being a duchess one day, do you not?"

"I do," the Duke replied. "Do you think your daughter would agree to it?"

Burrton grinned, his eyes shining with delight at the Duke's acceptance of his proposal. "I think she will do what she is told," he exclaimed, chuckling. "What of your son?"

Hesitating, Ware looked back at his old friend and pursed his lips. "Daniel may take a little … persuading, but I will do what I have to. Typically, it's my wife meddling in our children's affairs, but Daniel will be duke one day, so I suppose I ought to see to him. It is far past time he takes a bride."

"Of course he must!" Lord Burrton exclaimed. "He is the heir to the dukedom. He ought to have been the first to marry."

Nodding, the Duke felt himself fill with a sudden and fierce resolution. Lord Burrton was right. Daniel should have been the first to marry, the first to produce a child, but instead, he was shutting himself away in his country home and refusing to engage with society in any way. As the current duke and also Daniel's father, Ware had let this go for too long, had been far too indulgent with his son.

"Very well," he said, firmly, the matter now decided. "I will have my solicitor draw up the contracts."

Lord Burrton nodded, raising his glass in a toast. "To the future."

The Duke of Ware followed suit, lifting his glass in return. "To the future," he agreed, before throwing his brandy back, draining every last drop.

CHAPTER 1

"**N**o!"

Daniel Harrington, Marquess of Ravenhall, sat bolt upright in bed, sweat trickling down his back as he struggled to catch his breath.

It had been the same nightmare, the same blood-soaked vision that had returned while he had been deep in sleep. Try as he might, he could not rid himself of it, and he wondered just how many years he would continue to be tortured by not just dreams, but memories that refused to leave him.

There came a quiet rap at the door. "My lord?"

It was his ever-faithful butler, Woodward, one of very few people who knew precisely why Daniel was so troubled.

"Come in, Woodward," he called, wiping the sweat off his brow. "What in the hell are you doing here so early?"

The butler did not smile as he set down the breakfast tray at the table in front of the fire before going to pull back the drapes. "The hour is actually fairly late, my lord," he replied calmly. "There is coffee for you, but I can fetch something stronger if you need."

Daniel considered it for a moment but then shook his

head, running a hand over his face to clear the fog. "It's fine. I'm fine."

"Is there anything else you may need, my lord?"

"No, not in the least," Daniel replied truthfully, not wanting even his staff to witness any weakness. "Go on, off with you. I'll be down shortly."

The butler inclined his head. "Very well. And shall I ask the valet to have the bath drawn for you in the next room as usual?"

It had become Daniel's custom, whenever he had such a nightmare, to have a bath as soon as he could afterward. It was to wash the sweat from his body, as though a physical cleansing would rid his mind of the vicious memories that had brought on the nightmares in the first place.

"Yes, thank you," he muttered, throwing back the bedsheets and rising on slightly unsteady legs. "Give me an hour or so before returning"

"Very good, my lord," came the reply as the butler made to leave. "May I also remind you that there are two letters sitting with your breakfast tray?"

"The ones I chose to ignore last evening?" Daniel asked, with a slight lift of his eyebrow.

"Yes, those two," Woodward replied, without even a hint of censure. He had been with Daniel for far too long to be affected by his ever-changing moods. He nodded and took his leave.

Daniel slumped in his chair, glad that the fire was lit, even though it looked to be a warm day outside. He was always chilled after one of his episodes, and it would take him at least an hour to regain some semblance of warmth in his bones.

Letting out a long breath, he poured himself a coffee and added a splash of cream, taking a sip immediately even though it scalded his lips. He needed the heat, needed the wakefulness that coffee would bring.

He would go a few days without the nightmare, and then just when he convinced himself that he had broken away, it returned with the force of a slam from a runaway carriage. He closed his eyes, fighting the vision, but it flooded his consciousness nonetheless. He was standing on the threshold of his home, his nerves on edge from the creak of the door swinging open on its hinges.

The dark of night followed him over the threshold into the entrance, where the flicker of a nearly spent candle cast just enough light for him to see his betrothed, Miss Laura Churston, lying on the floor, blood pooled around her head while her eyes remained open and staring at him. Her expression was one of surprise, of such profound shock, that for a moment, Daniel had expected her to move, to scream, to do anything other than just lie there.

It was always the very same memory playing out in exactly the same way it had happened. His friend, Lord Hudson, had followed him into the house and urged him to leave the dead young lady alone, but Daniel had been unable to do so. Falling to his knees, he had cradled Laura's broken body in his arms, blood staining his hands, his clothes, his very soul. The authorities had come soon afterward and everything else had grown hazy.

Taking another sip of his coffee, Daniel closed his eyes and tried to thrust the pictures from his mind, but as usual he could not easily do so. It took a great deal of effort to force them to fade, and he found himself wishing he could remember Laura as she had been in life — elegant, refined, and beautiful. Instead, whenever he thought of her, all he could see was her bloodied body on the floor of his house, her eyes wide and staring.

Groaning, Daniel straightened his seat and threw his

head back, his gaze upon the ceiling as he attempted to push it all away.

He vowed that never again would he allow himself to love, for it was not worth the price of the pain that remained when it was taken away.

"I will find him," Daniel whispered, savagely. "I will have my revenge."

But first, more mundane matters. He found the letters, grimacing as he did so. One was from his solicitor, which he did not particularly care about, for it would, most likely, simply be some information on his holdings, while the other was from his father. He recognized the seal and knew that he ought to open it, as much as he dreaded it. His father had been trying to worm his way back into Daniel's life for some time, trying to get through the wall that Daniel had built up around himself, but Daniel was unwilling to allow him entry. He had no interest in taking up his responsibilities to the title again. He had far more important work to complete, which his father could never understand.

Possibly because his parents didn't know the truth about Laura. All been very carefully covered up, as requested by her father, Lord Stawell himself, the moment he had arrived at Daniel's home, having been sent for by one of Daniel's footmen.

Lord Stawell had not wanted all and sundry to know the horrific details of his daughter's death. He had told Daniel think of his future wife and children, that the stain of this could spread to them if he was not careful. Daniel had no interest anymore in marrying, nor creating heirs, but he had four siblings whose lives could be greatly affected.

And so, it had all been very neatly, very discreetly, taken care of, dismissed as an unfortunate accident — nothing more.

Daniel could still remember attending the funeral in a

state of shock, feeling numb and disconnected from everything and everyone around him.

He'd retreated to his estate, where he had stayed for the past six years.

Daniel broke the seal and unfolded the letter, recognizing his father's familiar scrawl across the page. Most likely, this would just be another plea for him to come to London for the Season, to find himself a bride and beget an heir. Daniel had no intention of doing anything of the sort. He noted the door opening as he picked up the letter, and he nodded as Woodward entered and began to clear away his breakfast dishes.

Son,

You are expected in London for the Season. As you sold your townhouse some years ago and appear not to have any intention of purchasing a new one, I have done so for you. As it happens, it is directly across from our own. Therefore, you will reside in your new townhouse and dine with your mother and me regularly. I expect you no later than a week this Friday.

Daniel snorted. This did not sound like his father, given that there were no questions, no mention of how quiet Daniel had been of late, nor even the suggestion that Daniel was able to refuse such a request. Given that he was of age, he had no need to obey his father, even though he did not want to anger the man unnecessarily. After all, it was not as though Daniel's solitude was the duke's fault.

"I have no intention of coming to London," Daniel said aloud to the letter as if his father could hear him. "Regardless of what you want, I will not be joining you and Mother for the Season."

"My lord?" came the reply, and Daniel started slightly as he realized Woodward was still in the room.

"My apologies, Woodward," he said. "I was speaking aloud. My father, it seems, forgets I am no longer a young lad, but a man grown, capable of making my own decisions."

It was a letter he would have to respond to but, since he did not feel any particular urge to do so at that very moment, Daniel set the letter aside and picked up the other.

Sighing, he opened the one from his solicitor, fully expecting to read something about one investment or another. What he read instead shocked him to the core.

Lord Ravenhall,

I have been tasked by your father to place a hold on your accounts for a time. As he still has control of your fortune, since it is, in fact, his wealth, I have had no alternative but to do so at once. I have been informed that it will be released to you again when your father wills it to be so. The address of your new townhouse is enclosed.

Yours, etc.

Daniel had to read the letter three times over before the truth finally registered, and he clenched his fingers into a fist around the paper until it was nothing but a ball. His father was manipulating him through his wealth in order to force his return to London. He would have little other option but to do so, for while his estate was his in name, all funds ran through his father's accounts, which would, one day, become his. Daniel had known this the day he had come of age, the day he had been given his own small estate and his father's secondary title, but he had never expected his father to use this knowledge in such a way as to manipulate him into doing what he wished.

"How dare you!" Daniel sputtered, throwing the letter across the room and leaping from his chair. Pacing back and forth, he shoved one hand into his hair, his eyes staring at nothing while he struggled to come to terms with his father's actions.

"My lord, may I be of assistance?" asked Woodward,

subtly reminding Daniel of his presence. He turned to look at his servant, seeing no fear in the man's eyes, and silently acknowledged he was one who truly knew him. Most men now approached him rather warily, if they did at all.

"No," he growled, just managing to catch his anger and frustration as they nearly boiled over while he raged inwardly as to what to do. Despite his turmoil, rational thought crept in as he accepted the truth. "There is nothing to be done. My father has quite firmly... requested... that I return to London for a time. Prepare everything for my departure within the week."

He was caught. If Daniel disobeyed his father, his work on behalf of those troubled souls he helped would have to cease. His estate was somewhat profitable, but it had only recently become so, and Daniel knew he could not sustain his activities while still paying his workers and purchasing required goods. Was this his way of forcing Daniel's hand, in an attempt to pull him from his life of solitude? The duke was typically a jovial sort, and, unless the situation was one which would cause hurt to his children, he left them to do as they pleased.

Apparently, something had changed. Daniel leaned heavily on the windowsill and looked out at the gardens below.

"Very well, my lord."

Letting out a long breath, Daniel rested his forehead against the cool glass in an attempt to quell his boiling fury. He had to ensure that when he found the man who had taken Laura, when he took his vengeance, it was discreet enough that his father, mother, and siblings would suffer no consequences.

"And once I find him," he whispered, his breath frosting the glass, "I will be free."

Closing his eyes for a moment, Daniel tried his best to

find the motivation he knew he needed to sit down at his writing desk and compose a letter to his father. A letter that would agree to what his father had asked of him. A letter that would force him to return to London to face his demons once more.

But just what would he do with them?

CHAPTER 2

"Christina?"

Miss Christina Princeton, daughter of the Marquess of Burrton, looked up from where she reclined on her favorite a leather-and-walnut chaise in the library.

"Ah, there you are," her father boomed, marching into the room with his usual grandiosity. "I've been looking everywhere for you."

Christina inwardly rolled her eyes at her father. He either paid no attention to her usual whereabouts, or he simply wanted to make a point, for she spent much of her time in this room and it should come as no surprise to find her here. The windows were large and overlooked the countryside, while the pale green of the walls had a calming feel to them that allowed Christina to escape into her favorite stories.

Showing respect, however, she set her book down and waited patiently for her father to either take a chair or to lean on the mantelpiece as he usually did when he had something to say. She remained seated as she looked up at her father, who was impeccably dressed as always, in direct contradiction to the wispy gray hair that flew about his head in every direction. His sharp eyes turned to her, causing butterflies take flight in Christina's stomach. Something was the matter. Something that she felt concerned her. Her father never looked at her with such attention. What was it he was going to say?

"Has this something to do with my future, Father?" she asked, a mixture of nerves and hope beginning to flutter in her chest. "Will you finally be taking me to London?"

He never spoke much of what was to become of her. He had yet to take her to London for a Season, though he'd promised to after her brother had been married. Christina knew that in her father's eyes she was not nearly as important nor deserving of as much consideration as her brother, but that didn't bother her so much as the lack of opportunity to determine what her fate might be.

Christina had heard her father mutter before that she read far too much and that she ought to be concentrating on how to better her looks, but she chose not to listen. She was never going to be beautiful in the way her father hoped. Perhaps that was the problem. He had always wanted to present his daughter as a 'diamond of the first water,' as he always said, but she had never quite managed to fulfil his expectations. She had the fair hair required for such a thing, yes, but her gray eyes, less than slender neck, and pronounced curves meant that she would never be heralded with such a title. It was not that she was ugly, she felt, but rather that she was perhaps a bit plain and a little plump — and no amount of curling her hair or having her maid apply a touch of rouge was ever going to change that. She had tried to avoid sweets, but it seemed no matter what she did, she always looked the same.

"My dear," her father boomed in his usual loud voice, ignoring her questions as if she hadn't spoken at all. "I have something of importance to tell you."

"Oh?" Christina murmured, putting her arms around her middle in an attempt to keep her breathing steady. "And what is that, Father?"

He tilted his head, a small smile spreading across his face that slightly relieved her nerves.

"I am to take you to London, my dear. For the Season."

Christina stared at her father for a long time, not quite sure what to say. She had been right! She had never thought it would happen. For years, her father had made a multitude of excuses as to why she could not go to London for the Season but now, finally, after all this time, she was to be allowed to go.

"Are you not going to say anything?" He beamed, looking at her with raised eyebrows. "I thought you would be pleased."

"I am *very* pleased," Christina breathed, her voice nothing more than a whisper as she allowed a smile to finally break across her face. "I — I can hardly believe it, Father!"

He chuckled. "I am sure you will make a marvelous impression, my dear. Not that it matters all that much, I must say."

The excitement faded somewhat as she looked at her father, noticing the gleam in his eye, and she studied him more carefully. Oh no, she realized, this was not just a simple trip to London in order to find herself a gentleman; there was more planned. She had seen that look in her father's eyes at another time. A time when he had been making arrangements for her brother.

"Father," she said slowly, sitting forward a little on the chaise as her book toppled off the arm of the lounger and fell to the floor. "What do you mean, it will not matter?"

The smile faded slightly from her father's expression as he looked back at her from where he now leaned heavily on the mantelpiece. "It is only that you need not worry about finding yourself a suitable gentleman, my dear, for I have found one for you."

Her world seemed to slow to a stop, freezing in place. This was not what she had expected. She had longed for a Season, longed for a time where she might meet and dance and converse with all manner of gentlemen, but it seemed, while she might still do so, she would not be given the opportunity to choose a husband for herself. She would not be courted, would not have the pleasure of being taken for carriage rides, to the theatre, or simply for a stroll in the park by a man she might herself have an interest in. It was already decided for her. Worst of all, she had no choice over the person she was to spend the rest of her life with. Perhaps if she had been prepared for this, it would have been easier to accept. But never had her father made mention of the fact that he had any interest in creating a match for her, and so she had allowed her imagination to fill with possibilities.

"I thought it best this way," her father continued some-what airily as though he had done her a wonderful favor. "You will not have the worry that you might not be... adequate enough to find a suitable gentleman."

Christina closed her eyes tightly, the familiar pain slicing through her before she could brush it away. Her father had, once again, gotten to the crux of the matter in his usual blunt way. He did not think her pretty enough to secure a gentle-man. He had told her so often that she was much too book-ish, that gentlemen did not wish for a bluestocking, but she had been unable to stop herself from learning all she could. Books opened up a world to her far beyond her home.

"You shall have new gowns and the like, of course, for a trousseau will be important," her father continued, waving his arms, gesticulating wildly now as he went on. "It is a wonderful match, my dear, much better than you could ever have secured for yourself. Why, the opportunity presented itself to me, and I seized the moment!"

He would never change, Christina thought with a sigh.

"A duke's son!" her father exclaimed, delivering his last piece of news with a broad smile and bright expression, as though she ought to be almost overwhelmed at what he had managed to achieve for her. He pushed away from the mantle, coming over to her and taking her by the shoulders. "My dear friend, the Duke of Ware, has a son of marriageable age, and it has all been arranged. You will do very well, Christina."

A ripple of anger began to make its way through Christina's frame, her eyes misting with sharp fury. He believed himself to have done a wonderful thing for her while robbing her of the dreams she'd harbored for so long.

"You will be a duchess one day!" the marquess exclaimed delightedly, letting her go and striding around the room, before turning back to look at her with a finger in the air and adding hurriedly, "Provided the son agrees, of course, which I'm certain he will."

"Agree?" Christina repeated, faintly, her anger now being replaced with confusion and a bit of suspicion. "What can you mean, Father? He doesn't *know*?"

He shrugged, as though it was not all that important, waving a hand. "The duke has yet to convince his son, that is all, but I am sure the marquess will do just as he is expected."

"But you cannot guarantee it," Christina replied, tears of frustration now forming in her eyes. "Father, how could you do this? If it becomes known that I have been turned down, then I will be shamed and no gentleman will want to come near me. What were you thinking?"

Her father held up his hand, stemming her torrent of words. "Christina, please. I have been careful to make all the arrangements properly. No one yet knows of this other than the duke and likely his family by now. Once you have met and courted, the banns will be posted and all will be well."

"But only if he agrees," Christina stated, seeing her father's answering nod. "And, given how poorly you think of me in terms of my beauty and my activities, what makes you think that he will do so?"

To her surprise, her father chuckled as though she had made some kind of joke. "Because, my dear, he is a recluse! He has not been in society for many years and has only been encouraged back due to his father's insistence. I am sure he will not mind what kind of bride he marries, so long as she is entirely suitable to be his wife — and you, my dear, have all of the necessary qualifications. You have manners and tact, and are very presentable."

Her breathing became ragged, her fingers lacing together so tightly that they hurt. She couldn't look at her father, her gaze resting on the intricate pattern of the green, gold, and cream Aubusson carpet at her feet as she tried to take it all in.

"The duke will convince him, I am sure of it," her father continued, nonchalantly. "Do not worry, my dear, all will be well. Ah, my daughter, a duchess!" He shook his head as though hardly able to believe it, beaming at her.

"When do we leave?" she asked, suddenly desperate for him to leave her alone so that she might consider her sudden change in circumstances. "Is it soon?"

"In two days' time," he replied, making his way toward the door. "And we have our first engagement in five days from now — a ball, at Lord Fauconberg's home. An old friend of mine, you see, who will be delighted to welcome you." He made his way toward the door, his smile never fading. "And you shall meet your betrothed there, that very night! I shall ensure that you have all you need to make an excellent first impression, my dear. He shall have no need to turn away from you."

Christina knew that she ought to thank her father for what he had done, was *expected* to thank him, but her mouth refused to form the words. She tried to nod, to smile, but her face was frozen in a state of astonishment.

"Yes, well…. I can see that this has come as a bit of a surprise," the marquess finished, clearing his throat as he opened the door. "I shall see you again at dinner this evening, Christina, and we can talk some more then, should you have any questions."

Christina nodded, looking down at her knuckles, now white from the tight grip of her hands clasped together as she looked away from him, her stomach swirling with sudden nausea. She did not say another word, waiting desperately for the sound of the door closing behind her father.

The gentle click of the handle told her that she was blessedly alone. Rising from her chair, she strode to the window and looked out at the scene before her, drinking it in as though it would revive her. If all went to her father's plan, she would not be calling this place home any longer. Her removal to London was not to be the exciting few months she had dreamed of but was instead suddenly filled with an unknown dread, for it meant an introduction to a man who had been chosen for her. Being a duchess meant nothing, for she had never had any wish to increase her status within society. All she had wanted was the chance to have a Season of her own, an opportunity to meet and consider gentlemen herself, to find a man who would share her interests, her joys, her penchant for life.

But it was not to be so.

Within a few minutes, she had learned that her life here was over. Whether she wanted to or not, it was her time to leave, time to move on with her life — except that her destination was not one of her own choosing. Her father had done the same for her as he had done with her brother — ordered and organized her life for her. Her brother had married, though from what she had seen, he was not altogether happy, choosing to spend most of his days separated from his wife.

She did not want the same for herself, and all because her father believed that she would not be able to attract a gentleman on her own. That tore at her heart, the thought of how her father saw her. Not good enough, not attractive enough, not respectable enough as a bluestocking, but — as he had said — her only redeeming qualities being that she was polite and presentable. Tears of anger and frustration poured from her eyes. The control of her life would pass from her father to her husband.

She had never felt so helpless, had never felt so alone — and there was nothing she could do to change it.

CHAPTER 3

*D*aniel shuddered as he stepped into his new home, trying not to recall what he had seen the last time he had stepped across the threshold of a London home. After ridding himself of his former townhouse, whenever he had been required to return to the city, he had always stayed at an inn or with Lord Hudson. It was not as though he hadn't the funds to keep it, but had considered it to be a useless investment, for he had no intention of spending any prolonged length of time in London.

"Thank you," he murmured, glad that he had been able to take his butler with him to London as he handed the man his hat and coat. Woodward, who had arrived a couple of days prior to Daniel to arrange everything for his stay, was near his father's age, but Daniel had always felt comfortable around him, even before the incident. "Are you sure they will be able to spare you back at Ravenhall Manor?"

The butler smiled, his eyes alight with a sudden spark of mirth. "I'd say so, my lord. That young footman will do very well in my place. In a year or so, I'm sure he'll be looking for a place of his own in another household. A proper butler

23

needs a proper domain, and he will be past the realms of a mere footman by then."

Daniel shot him a rueful smile. "Well, I do rather monopolize your time, do I not? I suppose it is rather a good thing that I have another man able to step into your shoes at short notice."

Woodward nodded, and Daniel was reminded of just how much he had come to depend on Woodward over the last few years. The man had not left his employ, not even after the horror that had been Laura's death, and he seemed to know precisely what Daniel needed. He was the only member of staff who was aware of Daniel's ongoing nightmares and ensured that he was very well looked after an episode left him weak.

"Should you like to change for this evening's dinner, my lord?" the butler asked, changing the conversation topic quickly.

Daniel's lip curled. "Ah, yes. Dinner with my parents? Across the street... how fortunate." He knew that sarcasm dripped from his words but did not hide it from his butler, who knew how much Daniel despised being ordered about.

"Indeed it is," Woodward calmly replied. "Shall I have the valet lay out your things?"

"I suppose you must."

The butler paused for a moment. "And Lord Hudson is waiting for you, my lord."

Daniel spun around at once. "Hudson? Here?" He knew Hudson had returned to London before Daniel himself had, but he had not expected to see him so quickly. A faint note of worry stirred, and Daniel hoped that nothing had gone awry.

"In the drawing room, my lord, although he told me to allow you to get settled before informing you that he was here."

"And I am very glad you ignored that missive," Daniel replied, taking a step forward. "Thank you, Woodward."

"You can find the room down this hall, through the first door on your right."

Daniel nodded and made his way down the corridor, which was lined with watercolors and a portrait of his grandfather. So his mother had been here. It was certainly not styled in Daniel's taste, but he had no plans to rectify the situation, as he did not intend on staying here long — only until he could convince his father of the folly of his decision.

Turning into the drawing room, Daniel's lip curled as he took in the feminine decor of the room, the floral arrangements and the colorful seating around an elegant sofa table. He couldn't help but grin, however, at the sight of his friend looking altogether uncomfortable seated in one of the over-stuffed chairs, brandy in hand.

"I see you've already helped yourself," Daniel chuckled, as he sat down opposite. "Just like you, Hudson."

"I think I deserve it," Lord Hudson muttered, not looking in any way pleased. "After what I've been through, I need more than one of these."

The smile left Daniel's face at once. "What happened?"

"Look, Ravenhall, I know what you — what *we* are trying to do is for the betterment of others, to seek justice for those who cannot find it for themselves, but my God, sometimes you wonder, is what we do making any difference at all?"

Daniel sighed, running a hand through his hair.

"I know it may seem that way, Hudson," he said. "But the way I see it, if I can help another poor soul find the justice I seek for myself, or even prevent it, then yes, for one person what seems like a small action can make a big difference."

"You know this will never satisfy your own loss," Hudson said quietly, and Daniel threw him what he hoped was a scathing look, but Hudson continued, as the only person other than Woodward who knew what Daniel had gone through, what he still saw many nights. "I understand your motives, Ravenhall, and I support what you are doing more than any other. But that doesn't mean I condone all of your methods."

Daniel remained silent, choosing not to answer his friend. Over the last year, he had put together a small group of men who reached out to others on his behalf, using his funds and his support. Daniel did not always get involved but allowed Lord Hudson to take most of the control. It meant that he was able to stay at Ravenhall Manor and take care of his own tenants and land, knowing that there was good being done in his name. Of course, at times he came down to London to involve himself, when it was required to take things further than his men were willing to go. The less time he spent in London, however, the less he battled his demons.

Thankfully, Lord Hudson was a viscount who had very little else to do, other than marry and create heirs, which he was not particularly inclined to do as yet. He'd always said he had a very charming, very practical younger brother who had already produced children of his own, so that there was nothing particularly urgent about his own matrimonial state. It seemed that, aside from their love of port and good books, both Daniel and Lord Hudson shared a sense of injustice for those of lesser means who needed help and protection. Hudson was involved practically, while Daniel, for the most part, took on the monetary issues. All in all, it was a beautiful partnership.

However, there were times when Hudson appeared to be rather discontented with what he had seen and what he had been required to do. Tonight appeared to be one of those moments.

Daniel watched carefully as Hudson threw back his glass of brandy, his expression dark.

"Hudson, what happened?" he asked again, a little abruptly. "Speak, man, and stop drinking yourself into a stupor."

Thankfully, Hudson appeared to hear him this time and shrugged. "It's all sorted now, Ravenhall, you will be glad to hear. I took a punch to the gut and had to drag one of those brutes of a husband along to the authorities, but it's nothing too much to bear. It was just seeing the state of those children." He shook his head, passing one hand over his eyes. "How can a man treat his own kin that way?"

Daniel felt his stomach tighten as he recalled that, during his last short visit to London, he had been told of a woman in need whose husband was drinking himself to death and neglecting his duties to his wife and children. Daniel had wanted to help, and Hudson had promised to look in on the lady. Apparently, it had been worse than Daniel had feared.

"They're safe now, of course," Hudson continued, settling Daniel's mind. "Put them in one of those houses you've rented, although by the looks of things, that one's almost full."

Daniel nodded slowly, his brow furrowing as he tried to think of what to do next. He had already rented three large homes in London, which he had proceeded to fill with those who had nowhere else to go. Each house had a small staff of its own, with the residents contributing to the cleaning and upkeep. Any disorderly behavior was swiftly dealt with. Two of the homes were solely inhabited by women and children, those who had been neglected or mistreated by their husbands and needed a place to stay — for a few days, months, or years, depending on the case.

"There is another house available near the others," Lord Hudson continued, helpfully. "Might you be interested in that?"

Daniel's expression cleared and he chuckled. "Yes indeed.

27

You know me far too well, Hudson. I should have sent you to my solicitors directly."

Lord Hudson managed a grin. "What makes you think I have not already dispatched a note to them?"

Rolling his eyes, Daniel pulled himself up from his chair and went to pour himself a drink, topping up Hudson's glass. "I am sorry it was a bad one, Hudson."

The man shrugged, feigning nonchalance. "It happens. You are a generous man, Ravenhall, although I am sorry that you were forced to return to London."

Daniel said nothing as he sat back down, though he shook his head. "I'm not a good man, Hudson," he said. "You know some of the things I have done."

"True, but—"

"The man who went after my brother and now sister-in-law, do you remember what happened to him? Or the sop who tried to force himself on my sister? News takes some time to reach me, but when it does … well. Let's simply say my anger sometimes gets the better of me."

Hudson looked down at his drink before lifting his head to meet Daniel's gaze.

"It doesn't have to be that way, Ravenhall. You can find justice without taking the life of another."

Daniel shrugged, and the familiar self-loathing crept through him as he clenched his teeth together. "It's not as though I have ever taken a life with my own hands, though I might as well have, as I have directly arranged it. It's only that I've not the courage to go through with it myself."

"You are here now, close to your family once more."

"Indeed. But I had no choice. I had to return else I would not be able to continue supporting those who require it."

"You could always tell your father what you are doing."

Daniel sat back and leaned his head against the chair. "You know I cannot. If I was to do so, then he would ask me why I felt I needed to do such things, which would only lead to questions about Laura. It would all come out in the end, and I would rather not speak of it."

Lord Hudson shrugged, his brown eyes flickering. "Mayhap it might do you a world of good to talk to someone about it. You hold it all in here," he said, tapping the side of his head. "You know that I would be willing to listen."

"What is there to say?" Daniel asked, narrowing his eyes at Hudson. "I am trying to forget it all. The only thing that will bring me any relief is the knowledge of Lord Northcliffe's whereabouts so that I might begin my pursuit of him." Daniel knew with certainty that Northcliffe was the one responsible. Woodward had opened the door that night to a gentleman, only to find himself shoved back hard as Lord Northcliffe slammed the door open, determined to get inside.

Such was the fervor in his heart that he did not realize he had clenched his fingers into a fist until Lord Hudson cleared his throat and nodded at his clasped hand.

"Your anger has simply grown over the years."

"Would yours not?" Daniel exclaimed, a little surprised at his friend's questions. They had been working together for some time and this was the first time in as many months that Hudson had challenged him.

Lord Hudson nodded slowly, his eyes thoughtful. "Yes, I am sure my anger would flourish, but what is it that you plan to do, Ravenhall? Kill the man? Exact justice in your own way?"

Daniel felt his stomach churn at the thought of placing his hands around another man's throat, of pulling a trigger or pushing a sword point home, but in this case, he would not send another to do the job for him. "The constable cannot do anything. There is no evidence other than the butler's testimony, and he is too loyal to be trustworthy to any other. Even the implement that was used to bludgeon her was gone."

"I am aware of all that," Lord Hudson replied, gently. "I know that it was dark, which is why no one saw a man covered in blood making his way from your home. I know that, most likely, he hailed a hackney before throwing everything in the Thames or burning it. I know that you believe it was Lord Northcliffe but that there is nothing to prove his guilt. But you need to let it go."

Daniel sniffed disparagingly, trying to pretend that he was not in any way affected by what his friend had said. "I don't need to talk to anyone, not even you. I know that you are trying to help me but there is nothing that talking will do in my vow to get justice for Laura."

"And how will you do that if you cannot have Lord Northcliffe convicted?"

"I don't plan on him being convicted."

"You cannot kill him, Ravenhall," Lord Hudson replied, his voice filled with a warning. "You will only then be as guilty as he is, and all will know it was you. If he is truly guilty of what you believe him to be, then you must get him to confess, else you are attempting to punish an innocent man."

Anger burst through Daniel's veins, and he threw himself out of his chair, brandy sloshing over the glass and onto his hand. "There can be no one else! Only Lord Northcliffe sought Laura's hand in marriage. Only Lord Northcliffe attempted to steal her away from my affections, and when she told him that she would not be persuaded, his attempts to pull her away grew all the more desperate. When we became engaged, I saw the look on his face when it was announced. He hated her. He hated me. He wanted nothing more than to have Laura to himself, and since he could not have what he desired, he took her away from me so that I could not have her either. He will pay for what he has done."

Lord Hudson shifted a little uncomfortably in his chair. "There is another reason I have come to speak with you, Ravenhall. Word has reached me that Lord Northcliffe has, in fact, returned to London, after many years away. I was not going to tell you, but it is better you be prepared."

A deep, unfurling rage seared itself through Daniel's soul as he stared at his friend.

"And I can already see your reaction," Lord Hudson continued with a heavy sigh. "You must learn to control your temper, Ravenhall, or you will be of no use. You are going to be in the same room as Northcliffe on multiple occasions, I am sure of it, and you cannot let your anger get the better of you."

Daniel began to sputter, only for Hudson to hold up one hand, stemming the flow of words threatening to come from Daniel's mouth.

"You are quite justified in feeling all this, I know," he continued, as Daniel began to pace up and down the room. "But to exact justice on this man, to have a confession from his lips, you must find a way to first be civil toward him — while making every effort not to engage with him at all. If you reveal your hand too early, then the *ton* will think worse of you and pity him for being so poorly treated." He leaned forward, halting Daniel in mid-pace, and froze him in his stare. "Do you understand what I am saying?"

Daniel wanted to rush from the room at this very moment, battling the urge to go in search of Lord Northcliffe at once, so that he might beat the man to a bloody pulp — but Lord Hudson's calm words began to infiltrate his fury.

"Yes," he managed to say through gritted teeth. "Yes, Hudson, I understand."

"Good," Lord Hudson replied, calmly. "Well, I'd best be

off. I'll call by tomorrow afternoon and we can discuss how things are going. You'd best hurry. Dinner with your father and mother, isn't it? And you certainly can't go looking like that." He threw Daniel a wry grin as he rose to his feet, making Daniel aware that he was trying his best to pull Daniel further away from his uncontrolled anger. "Best to take things one step at a time, old boy."

"Indeed," Daniel gritted out, his hands slowly beginning to unfurl as he tried to get a rein on his temper. "Thank you, Hudson."

"Not at all," his friend replied opening the door. "Like I said, I'll be back tomorrow. Can't wait to hear why your father has summoned you back to London after all this time. Good luck!"

CHAPTER 4

ide-eyed, Christina glanced around her as the carriage traversed the streets of London. It had been so long since she had been to town, she felt like a foreigner. She was used to the great expanses and the open air of the country, and she felt somewhat stifled here, though her senses had never been so alert.

Perhaps it would be different in the light of the day. Her father had wanted to arrive in time to attend the theatre, to which Christina had readily agreed. He had assured her that her betrothed would not be in attendance, about which she was somewhat relieved. She would prefer some time to get used to the idea, to become acquainted with the city before she had to spend time in his presence.

The carriage pulled up in front of a stately home, and Christina looked across the seat at her father, her eyes narrowing as she took him in.

"Father?" she said with suspicion. "This is not some form of trickery, is it?"

"No," he chuckled. "It is not. Christina, there is one thing I haven't told you. I—"

"Lord Burrton!" a voice warbled, and Christina turned abruptly to the door of the carriage. "I know I should have waited inside, however, I simply could not help myself but hurry out to meet your daughter!"

Christina hurriedly closed her mouth when she realized it was agape, but she couldn't help from swiveling her head back and forth between her father and the elaborately clad woman standing in the carriage doorway, who was now looking at her father with a pout on her face.

"Are you not going to help me in?" she asked, and Christina could hardly get over the heavy hand the woman had taken to the color on her face. Her father finally bumbled over to her, helping her into the carriage. Christina nearly couldn't breathe, such was the overpowering scent of the woman's perfume.

"Christina, my dear, this is Lady Aster," said her father, his grin stretching wide, and the woman smiled broadly at Christina. Ah, Christina thought, this explained a lot. Her father was trying to be rid of her to make room for a new woman in his life.

"How lovely to meet you," she finally managed and was grateful the carriage ride to Covent Garden was short.

Lady Aster turned out to be not the worst sort of woman, though not the type that Christina could spend much time with. She trilled on and on, through the carriage ride, the theatre lobby, and up the stairs to their box. She seemed genuinely pleased to spend time with Christina, who soon realized that it was not Lady Aster who wanted her out of their lives, but her father himself.

He nearly ignored Christina, instead concentrating on the woman on his arm. When intermission finally came, Christina excused herself as quickly as she could, stumbling out of the booth in her haste. As she parted the curtains, she nearly ran into another woman, managing to right herself just in time.

"Pardon me—"

"I say, did you come out of the Marquess of Burrton's booth?" The woman asked, surprising her, and Christina felt her eyebrows rise.

"Well, yes, as a matter of fact, however—"

The young blonde woman interrupted her once more, shocking Christina further when a grin broke out on her face and she began motioning behind her for someone else to join them. "You must be his daughter! Oh, how lovely. Sebastian! Sebastian, come meet Lady Christina."

However did these people know her name? Christina found her nerves on edge as she stared openly at the woman, who was beautiful, her light locks the color of a field of wheat, unlike Christina's own hue, which was somewhere between blonde and a plain brown. She looked around her for a means of escape, but the woman grasped her hand between hers, bringing it excitedly to her breast.

"Oh!" Christina exclaimed before the woman turned to the man who had joined her. He seemed much more serious than she, though he had a light to his eyes, especially when he looked at the woman who was most certainly his wife.

"Lady Christina, I had so hoped to run into you," the woman said, to which her husband laughed.

"My apologies, but as you may have gathered by now, this is not a coincidence, my lady," he said. "My wife practically stationed herself outside your box before the first act was done."

"Do hush, Sebastian," she said, scolding him, before turning back to Christina and continuing in what could be described as a whisper, although Christina was certain nearly anyone walking by could hear. "Now, as we are to be sisters soon, we have so much to get to know about one another."

"Pardon me?" Christina's stomach dropped, and she looked closer at the woman. Oh dear. This must be—

"My brother is the Marquess of Ravenhall!" she continued. "Ever since my mother told me of your betrothal, I have been so curious to meet you."

The man she called Sebastian put his hand on his wife's arm, stilling her movements.

"Polly," he said gently. "Perhaps we should allow Lady Christina a moment," he said, before turning to Christina. "We only learned of your arrangement — not betrothal, Polly — this morning. I am not sure that the marquess himself is even aware as of yet, as he is just arriving in town this evening. It has been some time since my wife has seen her brother, so you can imagine her excitement. Allow me to properly introduce ourselves. We are Lord and Lady Taylor."

"But Polly to you, of course," Lady Taylor said, her smile never wavering. "Now come," she said, taking Christina's arm. "I would so love to know more about you."

As Christina allowed herself to be led down the corridor, she considered that, while this woman was perhaps slightly overwhelming in her exuberance, if all of the Harrington family was so welcoming, it might not be such a bad arrangement after all.

THREE HOURS AFTER LEAVING HUDSON, Daniel found himself sitting at the dinner table with his father and mother, who acted as though everything was just as should be expected. They had both warmly welcomed him and, while Daniel could admit that despite his misgivings he had been glad to see them, he could not help but remain somewhat distant due to how he had been summoned.

"I have missed you so very much these last few months,"

his mother commented as they finished their dessert. "With every other one of your siblings married, it has taken me a great deal of time to become used to living in such a quiet house. Ah, well. All is as it should be."

Daniel, who had put up with enough insipid conversation during dinner, cleared his throat as the footmen took the dishes away. "Are we to stay for a port, Father? I think you are aware, despite the warmth of your welcome and plentiful conversation, that there is something for us to discuss."

Much to Daniel's surprise, the duke did not appear to be in the least bit disconcerted by his frosty tone but rather smiled. That smile, in turn, made Daniel's frustration grow as he kept his gaze firmly fixed on his father.

"Of course, Ravenhall," the Duke replied calmly, startling Daniel with the use of his title. His father typically was not quite so formal in private settings. "We can discuss whatever you wish, although your mother is to remain a part of the conversation."

Blinking, Daniel turned to see his mother smiling back at his father as though this was quite to be expected.

"Mother, you knew about this?" he asked, somewhat taken aback that they had conspired against him.

"About what, my dear?" his mother asked, calmly, as the tea tray was set in front of her, though she was unable to keep her bright eyes and smile from him. "That you were to return to London? Yes, of course I knew."

"Not that," Daniel grated, becoming increasingly irritated with his parents' lack of serious regard for what they had done. "But that Father forced me to return to London."

His mother raised one eyebrow, no look of astonishment in her eyes. "Daniel, dear," she chided gently. "Wait until we are alone, please."

Daniel made to retort, only to catch the glint in his father's eye. He was being foolish in speaking so openly when the staff was still about, aware that gossip was one thing his father refused to tolerate. It was best not to say anything until the last footman was gone.

It gave Daniel time to calm his fractious nerves as he waited for the footman to close the door and leave them alone. He took the opportunity to study his parents, seeing his mother, as elegant as ever, with a calm smile on her face as though there was nothing untoward about the situation. His father was not in any way upset by Daniel's outburst but was instead pouring himself a somewhat large glass of port, and then another for Daniel.

"Now," the duke began, as the door closed tight. "Daniel, you have every right to be. However, I will not accept that I have done anything wrong in this. You have duties to the family, and they are duties you have not taken seriously. You have refused to answer my request to come to London and secure yourself a bride, instead insisting that you remain in the country."

"I know you cared for Laura very much," his mother added softly, placing a hand on his arm that he forced himself not to shrug off, as her face was awash with sympathy, "but that was years ago. You must let her go, put her memory to rest so that you might move on and find another. You need not love her, but you must do your duty regardless."

The very notion made Daniel's anger burn hotter, and he thumped the table with his fist, hard enough to startle his mother.

"I will not be told what to do!"

"Oh yes, you will," the duke replied, his voice calm yet steady. "You will, Daniel, and you will not speak to your mother like that. You are not a child any longer. We have given you plenty of time to find your own way, but this has gone on long enough. I will not have the future of our family line put in jeopardy by your selfish actions."

"Selfish!" Daniel exclaimed as blood roared in his ears. He pushed back from the table and began to pace around the room. "I have been nothing if not selfless these last few years! I have given myself to good works, have looked after my tenants and my lands with all the attention I could muster. My estate has been profitable because of the work I have put into it. I have not been in London drinking and gambling and chasing the ladies of the night simply so that I might enjoy myself. How dare you call me selfish in choosing not to find a bride until I am ready?"

There was a long, pronounced silence as Daniel's words echoed around the room. His mother was watching him closely, her eyes glistening with unshed tears, while the duke was rubbing his graying beard thoughtfully, sitting back in his chair and regarding Daniel.

"You are quite right, son," he said, after a long time. "I ought not to have called you selfish — but the truth is, I know very little about your life and what you choose to do with it. While you are doing all you can to look after your land and estate, which I credit you for, you are still neglectful of the one other duty you have been called to."

"The duty of matrimony to produce the heir," Daniel replied dully, his head hanging low as the fight went out of him. "I have brothers," he said as he sat back at the table.

"Thomas is at sea with no intention of returning," his father said. "He has two daughters and no sons. There would be nothing more selfish than to force Thomas's family to London, you know that, Daniel. Benjamin has made something of himself, it is true, but neither he nor his wife have any wish to take on the role of duke and duchess. As of now, they have no children. Perhaps in time they will, but it would be better were the line to continue from you — that a child grows up learning from his father, as you did."

The words echoed around Daniel's head. How ironic, that of three sons, none had any wish to take on the role of duke one day. His father was right, however. If he wanted to look after his family, there was no other way than to take on the role expected of him. His father was still the duke and he still the heir apparent. Deep within him, he heard a voice reminding him that his father was doing what he thought was best for Daniel and best for the title, but he chose not to listen to it.

"I did what I had to in order to force you to come to London for the Season," the Duke continued, quietly, "and my decision does not change. You are here for one reason and one reason only."

Daniel looked up, his heart thudding painfully. "And that is...?"

"To meet your betrothed," the duke replied, his eyes holding steady. "And to court her until your wedding day."

CHAPTER 5

"*R*avenhall, you look as though you are about to attend a hanging."

Daniel looked at himself in the mirror, seeing the lines on his face and the tenseness about his stature. "I don't know what you mean, Hudson," he muttered, as his friend chuckled all the more. "I think the ball this evening will be a wonderful event."

"Is that so?" Lord Hudson grinned, his eyes bright with laughter. "My goodness, Ravenhall, you cannot even muster up a modicum of interest, can you?"

Daniel drew in a long breath, turning away from the mirror that hung on the wall of the drawing room as he shrugged toward Hudson, who was reclining in the over-stuffed floral chair once again. "I do not think I need to."

"Because you're now betrothed."

Nodding, Daniel sat down heavily. "Precisely. There is no requirement for me to show any enthusiasm of any sort because the woman I am to marry will wed me regardless of whether I smile or frown this evening. Perhaps that is the one benefit of this arrangement."

It had been three days since Daniel had heard the news that he was to marry and he had yet to find a way to escape his sentence.

"I still can't quite get over it," he muttered, smoothing a wrinkle out of his carefully tied cravat. "I can hardly imagine marrying, let alone someone I have never met."

"What if she is ugly?" Hudson contemplated, and Daniel rolled his eyes as he accepted a drink from his friend.

"I doubt that. I have to take her to bed and, given how much my father wants the heir to be produced, I doubt he would saddle me with an unattractive wife."

Lord Hudson grinned, sending a ripple of irritation through Daniel. His friend was enjoying this situation far too much for Daniel's liking.

"And she has agreed to all this, I presume? You are not going to have some flighty young thing changing her mind the moment you scowl at her?"

Daniel snorted, loudly. "I highly doubt it. She is to be the Duchess of Ware one day. What kind of young lady turns such a title down?"

Hudson nodded slowly, his smile fading. "You do not mean to attempt to scare her away, do you now, Ravenhall?"

"I am angry, true," Daniel replied, crossing his arms. "It is not what I wanted — not yet anyway. I have my own life to lead, and now it seems as though my father is desperate to take that away from me. Besides that, after Laura… well. I do not think I will prove to be the husband this young woman is looking for. I shall not pretend to be someone I am not, however, and if she still wants me once she knows the way of it, then so be it."

"Your father is desperate to maintain the family line, as you yourself will be one day," Lord Hudson replied, firmly. "Besides, many gentlemen find themselves in your situation and do very well out of it. It takes a great deal of effort to secure a wife, you know. You should be relieved that you do not have to parade yourself through society and choose a lady for yourself! The moment you set foot at a social event, they will be swarming around you like river rats, all seeking to cling to you."

"And only interested in me because of my wealth and title," Daniel finished, with a dullness settling into his voice. "Yes, I know." A memory of his entry into societal events rose, of the days when he enjoyed the attention, though it had been caught by one beautiful woman in particular, who had loved him for who he was and not the title he held.

At least, that was what she'd always told him and he'd always believed it since he loved her in return.

Overwhelmed by frustration, he thrust to his feet and stormed toward the door, growing angrier with himself with each step. He'd never before questioned Laura's words, nor her affection for him, so why was he doing it now? Was it because he was to find himself married in a few short weeks? Or was it because he was growing colder and more cynical as the years passed, burying himself in his hatred of Lord Northcliffe?

"No more dawdling," he said sharply, as Lord Hudson stared at him in surprise. "Let's go. The last thing I want is my father to complain that I am late."

Hudson shrugged, threw back the rest of his brandy, and set the glass down. "As you wish," he murmured, eyeing Daniel carefully. "Are you sure you're all right, Ravenhall?"

"Yes," Daniel replied, tightly. "Let's go."

THE BALL WAS ALREADY in full swing by the time Daniel and Hudson arrived. While the sight of lords and ladies in all of their finery twirling around the room in front of them made

Lord Hudson grin, it filled Daniel with a certain amount of dread.

"Capital!" Lord Hudson exclaimed, rubbing his hands. "This should do me very well. Lots of young ladies to dance with, plenty to drink, and a card room should it all get too much."

He slapped Daniel on the shoulder, trying to get him to smile. "Stop looking so beastly or you will frighten away your bride long before she has the chance to get to know you," he continued, as they joined the line to greet their hosts. "You have to try to smile a little bit, Daniel. The poor creature's going to be terrified of you."

Daniel didn't care. He hated this, hated being here and being so on display. Turning his attention to Lord and Lady Fauconberg, he thanked them for their invitation and commented on how beautifully the room was decorated, how elegant Lady Fauconberg looked, and how wonderfully the orchestra played. The contrived words came easily to his lips, as he was fully in the knowledge that he was expected to give such compliments before excusing himself. It was how a gentleman such as he was meant to conduct himself and while his feelings on the role had changed, Daniel had never forgotten his training.

"Thank you, Lord Ravenhall," Lord Fauconberg murmured, as Daniel made to step away. "I do hope you have a *very* enjoyable evening."

There was a glimmer of a smile on the man's face, which Daniel caught just as he turned away. A heaviness settled in his chest. Apparently, Lord Fauconberg was aware of what Daniel was here for — and if Lord Fauconberg knew, then his wife knew too, and that meant within a day or two, London would be alive with the news that Daniel, the Marquess of Ravenhall and heir apparent to the Duke of Ware, was engaged.

He swallowed, hard. It was all becoming too much.

"Courage, man," Lord Hudson murmured, coming to stand by him. "I'm sure your young lady is very lovely and you will be more than happy with her. First meetings are always difficult. Just smile and say something to compliment her, request to dance and then leave her be. That will satisfy everyone and allow you to take things slowly."

Daniel made to reply as they came to the grand staircase which would lead them down into the ballroom, but, in that one moment, his whole being froze.

He could not speak. He could not move. His hands tightened into fists, his teeth ground together, his feet felt stuck to the floor. All he could see was Lord Northcliffe, smiling, laughing, and genuinely enjoying himself, as he stood in the center of the room.

"Ravenhall?" Lord Hudson said, quietly, nudging him. "Whatever's the matter? Don't tell me you've lost your nerve! It's only a woman."

Daniel tried to shake his head, his mouth opening and closing, but still, he could not say a word. Lord Northcliffe was some distance away but, from where he stood, Daniel was certain it was him. Six years he had waited for this, to come face-to-face with the man who had ruined his life.

"There," Daniel ground out, one finger stretching out to point at the man. "That is Northcliffe, is it not?"

Hudson's smile faded rapidly and he turned to look where Daniel pointed.

"I do not think it is," he said, slowly, his eyes turning toward Daniel before he looked back out across the crowd. "I will confess that the gentleman looks like him but I cannot be certain. It has been quite some time since I last saw him."

"It is him," Daniel ground out. "I would know him anywhere!"

White-hot anger began to race through him, his rage

spiking as he hurried down the steps into the ballroom, not even thinking about who might be watching his entrance. All he thought of was Northcliffe, all he wanted was to get to him — although what he intended to do once he did, Daniel had no idea.

"Ravenhall!"

Hudson grasped his arm tightly, pulling him back.

"What are you doing?" he hissed, dragging Daniel away from his quarry. "You cannot just go up to him in the middle of the ballroom!"

"Leave me be," Daniel exclaimed, not caring who heard him.

His friend shook his head, his gaze resolute. "For your own sake, I cannot do that, Ravenhall. Think about what you're doing! You promised me you would not act without proof."

Despite that, despite knowing that he ought not to go anywhere near Northcliffe, Daniel could not stop himself. "I must," he grated, shaking his arm free of Hudson. "You do not understand."

Leaving Hudson behind, Daniel hurried through the crowd once more, ignoring those who tried to greet him. His mind was filled with one firm purpose, his thoughts aimed in only one direction.

"Lord Northcliffe?" he gasped, his breathing ragged as he reached the group of gentlemen he had seen talking with the man, but found him nowhere in sight.

One of the gentlemen looked at Daniel in surprise, while the others began to whisper among themselves, shooting glances toward Daniel, some amused, others somewhat fearful.

"Lord Northcliffe just left us," one man finally said quietly, looking at Daniel with something like surprise. "He stepped out to the gardens."

Daniel turned away without a word, going straight toward the doors that led out to Lord Fauconberg's gardens. They would be well lit, he was certain of it, which meant that all he had to do was step out and find him there. Perhaps outside was better. He would draw less attention when he smashed Lord Northcliffe's face into the dirt.

The outside air was cool, rushing across his heated cheeks and somewhat calming his frantic thoughts. Daniel hesitated for a moment as he hurried down the steps toward the garden paths, stopping to lean against the stone wall as he collected himself.

What was he doing? What did he intend to do? Was he really going to beat Lord Northcliffe to a bloody pulp right here in Lord Fauconberg's gardens? Who would bear the brunt of his shame when it was discovered that he was responsible? He might feel vindicated, even relieved, but the truth would come out sooner or later and the *ton* would not understand his actions. He could try and explain but they would not listen. Rumors and gossip would fly all about and damage his reputation irreversibly. And not only his.

His father would be shamed. His mother would lose her standing in society, dropped like a hot coal from her circle of friends. His betrothed — whoever she was — would never be able to enter London without whispers about his behavior swirling around her. His children, should he have any, would never be allowed to forget the stories about their father.

But still, he could not simply let Northcliffe get away. He had to at least let the man know he was watching him.

Pushing himself away from the wall, Daniel hurried down the garden path, not seeing anyone about until his shoulder slammed into another person.

"Out of my way!" he snarled without so much as a look back, before dashing off into the darkness.

CHAPTER 6

Christina tried to catch her breath after the gentleman hurried away on the poorly lit garden path, her chest and shoulder aching where his body had slammed, hard, into hers. He had come from nowhere, rushing down the path with such abandon that Christina hadn't seen him until he charged headlong into her. And yet he had the audacity to tell *her* to move!

"Goodness, Christina!" her friend exclaimed from beside her, holding out a steadying hand. "Are you quite all right? Did you see who that brute of a man was?"

Christina took a few moments to catch her breath, holding onto Lady Beatrice's arm.

"I have no idea, but I have no intention of letting him speak to me in such a way!" she exclaimed, fury rising as the pain abated, and she turned around to peer into the darkness. "I must go and find him and tell him exactly that."

"No, we must *not*!" Lady Beatrice cried, catching Christina's hand. "It would be altogether untoward, and besides that, the waltz is starting soon, and you know how I love to dance. I have a set with Lord Heatheringhall, and Mother will be quite upset if I stand him up."

"You are right. You must go dance, and I will return shortly," Christina urged. "I will be but a moment."

"I cannot leave you," Lady Beatrice replied, shaking her head. "What if you are found, alone, with a gentleman in the darkness? It is not done. Your reputation will be sullied."

Christina did not care, especially since she was already engaged, and her betrothed had yet to present himself to her. He was clearly in no rush to meet her, as he had not even yet appeared this evening. Besides that, what was he going to do — break off their engagement? "I will simply take a moment to compose myself, and then I will make sure to slip back inside quietly. No one will be the wiser."

She smiled at her friend, glad that Lady Beatrice was showing her such consideration yet determined to call out whoever it was that had knocked into her without any kind of apology. "Thank you, Beatrice. I will not be long, I assure you."

She watched as Beatrice nodded slowly, a look of concern in her expression, before she made her way toward the door that led back into the ballroom. Even though they had only been in London for a few short days, Christina's father, the marquess, had made every effort to find her a friend or two. Thankfully, Lady Beatrice Jamieson, daughter of the Earl of Broughton, had been warm and welcoming from the moment Christina had been introduced to her, and they had seen one another every day since their first meeting. They were as different as could be in appearance. Lady Beatrice had jet black hair, always piled high on her head, and was short of stature, but she made up for it with an exuberant character. She was always ready with a smile, a quick comment or a joke that made Christina laugh, pulling her out of the doldrums she'd found herself in ever since her father had told her she was engaged.

Moving rapidly down the path, Christina's heart quickened as the darkness pulled her in. This part of the garden was much dimmer, although Christina did not want to think as to why that might be. Her cheeks burned with embarrassment as she hoped desperately that the gentleman she was pursuing did not think she was seeking him out for some kind of liaison.

"Excuse me!" she called, seeing a shadowy figure moving quickly up ahead, dodging the light of a lone lantern. "I say, stop for a moment, if you please. I must speak with you." Her frustration at being treated in such a rude manner began to rise all the more as the gentleman ignored her entirely, despite the fact that Christina was sure he could hear her call out to him.

"Stop — you there!" she called again, only to gasp aloud as the gentleman reached another she had not seen, and without stopping, launched himself at the man, throwing a punch at him.

"How dare you show your face!" The first gentleman shouted as Christina began to stagger back, her hands pressed to her mouth as she tried to hide. "I have been searching for you for six years. Six years! Do *not* think that I intend to let you get away now."

Christina did not know what to do. She tried to move so that she might turn around and hurry away, but her feet appeared to be fastened to the ground.

"I will do all I can to destroy you," she heard the gentleman say, his voice loud yet rasping. "You do not deserve to live!"

"Then kill me," came the second man's voice, filled with an arrogance that made Christina wince. A man ought not to speak like that when he was being threatened, not if he wanted to get away with his life. The first gentleman was clearly in a state of furious rage for whatever reason, so surely it was best not to frustrate him further?

"Believe me, I want to," the first gentleman continued, his hands grasping the second gentleman's collar as he dragged him up to his tiptoes. "I want to put my hands around your throat and squeeze until the life goes out of your eyes."

Christina gasped, horrified, wanting to move yet fixed on the scene in front of her. She grabbed hold of the back of a bench that sat just beside the path. This gentleman, whoever he was, was clearly unstable. Threatening to kill a man in cold blood — in the middle of a ball, no less?

"I will do whatever I have to in order to get you to confess," she heard the first man say, as the second man let out a groan of pain. "But it will not be a physical punishment. I will not let your crimes sully my own reputation, nor that of my father's. Do not doubt, for one moment, that you will be able to continue with your life as though everything is just as it seems. I know what you did, and I will prove it."

Christina sank behind the bench as the sound of a punch meeting its mark reached her ears. Glancing over at them, she saw that the second man was now doubled over, his hands clutching his stomach as the first man finally released his quarry, striding away from him.

Stay still, Christina told herself, trying to make herself as small as possible as she crouched behind the bench. *He might not see you.*

Unfortunately for her, the gentleman started in surprise as he stopped next to her, and she cursed her silvery white gown. As beautiful as it was, hugging her curves and then cascading in folds down her waist, it must have shimmered in the moonlight, giving her away.

"What are you doing here?" he growled, striding toward her, as though he knew who she was. As he neared, the lantern caught his face, and Christina was taken aback by the hard edges of his features, at the way his lip curled in a near snarl. He would have been good looking, with his strong jawline, high forehead, and the whisper of hair across his chin, but his anger masked it all. She stood but shrank back, as if the darkness could keep her from him. "Why are you out here, alone?" he snapped at her.

"Do excuse me," Christina replied, whispering despite her best attempts to speak with confidence. "I— I simply—" *Compose yourself, Christina.* She straightened her shoulders as she strengthened her voice. "I needed to speak with you. To tell you how horribly you behaved yourself when you hit me on the path. However...."

He stepped closer until he was standing but a foot from her, and Christina could not bring herself to look up into his face, hating that she began to tremble. She clenched her hands together to stop.

"You witnessed that?" The gentleman asked, calmer now, still looking down at her. Christina was a tall woman, but this man towered above her. "It is not what you think, my lady. We had a gentleman's quarrel, of a very serious nature."

Christina swallowed hard, wishing he would leave. "I am sure it is none of my business."

"Then why did you not go inside?"

Christina felt her skin prickle with tension, her throat working hard as she battled to keep her composure. "As I said, I needed to speak with you, and was... shocked by what I saw."

She refused to tell him that part of the reason was that her limbs were too weak to move, and her fingers tightened together as she fought to remain calm.

"Then allow me to now escort you back inside."

"No!"

She jerked away from him as he bent down, resisting his

touch. She had stayed far enough in the dark that she hoped he hadn't seen her face, that she wouldn't have to admit knowing him were she to ever see him again.

"Please," he said, firmly, his face now just as swathed in shadow. "You cannot stay here alone."

"I will do as I please," Christina replied, her voice now hoarse and rasping. "I have no need for your company."

To her horror, the gentleman suddenly grasped her arm tightly and, despite her unwillingness, she found herself walking alongside him, over the path and away from it.

"Be silent, please," he whispered, as he led her into the deeper shadows of the trees surrounding the path, hiding them both entirely. "You must not say a word."

Christina fought her fear, her eyes wide as he pressed her back against the trunk of a very large tree, her breathing now ragged. She could sense that his face was but inches from hers now as he held close.

"I'm not going to hurt you," he promised, as a small whimper left her lips. "I just cannot allow you — nor I, for that matter — to be seen."

"And why is that?" Christina whispered, her hands tightening together again as he stepped back slightly now, leaving only one hand on her arm. "Because you do not want the *ton* to know that you are a cruel man with a penchant for dealing out punishment where there has been no crime?"

He growled, his hand tightening on her arm, and Christina flinched as though he might strike her.

"I have done nothing wrong," he said firmly, his voice a little louder than a whisper. "That gentleman has got only the very first taste of what I have planned. He deserves far worse."

Christina swallowed hard, feeling tears prick at her eyes as she tried her best to understand what this man was saying. "What has he done to deserve this?" she whispered, feeling the bark of the tree rub against her skin. "Stolen a lady from under your nose? Beaten you at cards one too many times?" Her tone became mocking, as her fear was replaced by anger at the way he was treating her, and her eyes filled with the memory of what she had seen. "A gentleman's quarrel, I believe you said."

Strong hands grasped her shoulders, and she flinched as he held her firmly.

"Do not mock me," he commanded, and she felt the puff of air brush across her cheek. A mixture of sweetness and spice that was likely port laced his breath. "And do not speak of what you do not know. That man took a life."

She froze for a moment, looking up at the shadowy figure who held her. She gasped suddenly as his face came into focus, the intensity of his crystal blue eyes bearing off into the distance. She studied him intently and found she was trapped now not by his arms, nor his body, but by the haunted look she saw in his eyes. Her attention was snapped, however, when she saw figures moving near them on the path, and she opened her mouth to call out to them for help.

And then, out of nowhere, before she could make a sound, his lips were on hers, catching her cry in his mouth. She was shocked by the softness of his kiss, so unlike the hardness of his face. Initially, it was apparent that he simply pressed his mouth to hers to keep her silent, but then, somehow, it all changed.

Christina did not know how it happened, or what to do once it did.

Her body was reacting in a way she'd never expected. It was growing warm, the icy fear beginning to fade away as she was kissed by a stranger, by the very man she'd been trying to escape from.

His lips were firm yet gentle, his arms coming around her waist as he pulled her tightly against him. She could feel the hard planes of his body as they pressed against the softness of hers, and she wondered at the fire beginning to burn deep within her. She had never been kissed before, had not entirely known what to expect, but this was far more than she could have ever imagined.

His tongue brushed against her lips, and she jumped, startled by the intimate intrusion. She should push him away, but instead, her body acted of its own will, her mouth opening up to his probing, allowing him inside. A whimper slipped out, only this time with passion as his tongue swept over hers, exploring, teasing. It was a sensation unlike anything she had ever experienced before, and she found herself clinging to his shoulders, pulling him in, wanting more of the forbidden fruit.

And then, just as quickly, she was standing on her own again, the stranger now a little away from her, having ripped their lips apart. She sagged back against the tree in order to remain upright, as she could hardly seem to stand for a moment. Her heart pounded a staccato beat.

"They're gone now," he said, with just a curl of distaste touching his words. "You can go."

Christina remained rooted against the tree, realizing what he'd done. He'd kissed her so that she wouldn't draw attention to them. There had been others walking nearby that he'd heard and, to silence her, he'd done the only thing he could — covered her lips with his own. She had not only allowed it, but she had *welcomed* it, had asked for more from him.

Shame leeched into her pores as she stumbled away from him, making her way through the gray darkness back to the path, hurrying up toward the house, patting at her hair and her clothing as she went to ensure all was in order.

Looking over her shoulder, she saw that the gentleman had followed her, although he now stood entirely motionless as she continued on her way. He cut an imposing figure, and she could still see his square jaw jutting out as he watched her go with something like frustration in his gaze.

She turned away, not caring who saw her as she climbed the steps and entered the ballroom once more.

"Christina!"

Lady Beatrice grasped her arm at once, pulling her away from the rest of the crowd to the side of the dance floor.

"I've been waiting for you for an age!" Lady Beatrice exclaimed as Christina tried her best to appear as though nothing had disconcerted her. "Are you quite all right?"

"Quite," Christina replied, in a voice she realized didn't quite match the false smile she plastered on her face. "I am sorry to have kept you waiting."

Lady Beatrice frowned as they walked, leading Christina toward a few empty chairs near one side of the ballroom. "Sit down, please. Are you sure you are all right? You look very pale."

Christina shrugged. "I should have listened to you. Being alone in the dark with a less than amiable gentleman was not my wisest idea."

Lady Beatrice gasped at Christina's admission, her blue-green eyes wide as could be. Christina tried to smile at her. Beatrice seemed to truly care about her well-being, despite the fact they had only recently become acquainted. "Never say he was rude to you!" she exclaimed.

Still feeling the imprint of his lips upon hers, Christina froze the half-smile on her face. "More than rude," she replied, softly. "Needless to say, I shall be very glad to never see him again."

CHAPTER 7

*I*t took Christina a good hour to feel more like herself, although she did not say anything further of the encounter to Lady Beatrice. It was not worth speaking out loud, she thought, aware that she would be bringing as much shame onto herself as onto the gentleman who had placed his mouth on hers.

She should never have gone to speak with him alone. Lady Beatrice had tried to warn her but she had been so angry with how he'd treated her that she'd ignored the good advice entirely.

Thank goodness no one had seen them in the gardens, for that would have made things all the more difficult for her, particularly since she was supposed to be nearly engaged. Her stomach dropped to her toes at the thought of what might have happened should they have been discovered, and a sheen of sweat broke out on her brow.

"I think your father is approaching, Christina," Lady Beatrice whispered, passing her a delicate lace handkerchief. "Dab your forehead and try to smile. He does look somewhat fierce."

Christina accepted the handkerchief and did as her friend instructed, although not for the reasons Lady Beatrice thought. "My father always looks that way, Lady Beatrice, but thank you. Do excuse me."

She rose to her feet and made her way toward her father, fully aware of what was to come. She had not spoken to Lady Beatrice about her engagement since it was not yet meant to reach the ears of the *ton*. She enjoyed Beatrice's company, but she couldn't be sure yet if she could trust her to keep such things to herself.

Now it seemed, she was to meet her betrothed for the first time. They would greet one another, talk for a few minutes, dance together, and then be on their way. It would not be overwhelming; her father had promised. She would have time afterward to consider all that had happened, to think about the gentleman before their next meeting the following evening at dinner. It sounded so simple, but this was truly monumental.

"You actually look quite nice this evening, my dear," the marquess boomed, as he offered her his arm. "We have a small room to the left, away from the other guests. Best to do this sort of thing quietly, don't you think?"

"Yes, Father," Christina replied, automatically.

"This way."

He led her through one door which opened to a long corridor, walking down it quickly as the sound of voices reached her ears. Christina's nerves jangled as they rounded the corner, only to see an older, distinguished couple standing there waiting. The gentleman was tall and distinguished, while the woman maintained a regal air, her dark locks streaked with a bit of gray, yet her beauty held firm.

"Your grace," her father said at once, giving the gentleman a small bow. "How good to see you." He led Christina forward, dropped her arm, and stretched his out toward her as if presenting a gift. "This is my daughter, Lady Christina Jamieson. Christina, this is the Duke and Duchess of Ware."

Christina executed the perfect curtsy, despite the hammering of her heart. "How very nice to meet you both," she said quietly, lifting her head and then, finally, her eyes toward them. They were both smiling at her, their faces kind. The Duke of Ware appeared to be the same age as her father and, while Christina knew her father had been friends with the duke for a long time, she had never met him before and he did not appear as she had pictured him. There was no arrogance written on his face, no lift of his chin as his gaze looked her up and down. Instead, his eyes were kind, and he wore a gentle smile on his face as he took his wife's arm. The duchess also made Christina feel at ease, her face holding nothing but sweetness. Despite her age, she seemed to exude youthfulness, her blue eyes bright as a warm smile settled on her face. What was it about those eyes that seemed so familiar?

"How very good to meet you at last, Lady Christina," the duchess said, kindly. "My goodness, it seems my husband is able to make a good decision after all! I should not have doubted you, my love," she continued, glancing over at her husband before turning back to Christina. "You, young lady, are the picture of perfection."

Not quite sure whether to be embarrassed or compli-mented, Christina chose to remain silent, her eyes flicking from one person to the next as she her cheeks warmed.

"Our son will be here to meet you in but a few moments. He is quite… eager," the duke continued quietly. "Just in here, my dear. We thought to allow you a few minutes alone so that there is no awkwardness."

"It is always strange to be introduced to one's betrothed in the company of others," the duchess replied, with a quiet laugh and a secret look at her husband. "I remember our introduction well."

Christina, feeling as though her limbs had turned to blocks of wood, thanked them all and stepped through the open door. She took a few steadying breaths and then chose to sit in a mahogany elbow chair facing the door, her back straight as she worked to maintain her composure. This was not what she had expected but perhaps it was for the best. To meet one's future husband in front of her father and his parents would have, indeed, been somewhat awkward.

She did not have time to consider it any longer, for another voice joined the others, snaking in through the open door toward her.

Christina felt her breath catch, her mind scrambling to place the voice as she stood and took a step toward the door in order to hear better. She knew it already. How was that possible? Had she met the duke's heir before?

"In here, Ravenhall," she heard the duke say. "Just a few minutes, mind you."

Christina lowered her head and curtsied the moment the door opened, hardly daring to look up. When she did so, she saw standing before her a tall, broad-shouldered gentleman with a shock of chestnut hair and a slight curl to his lips, as though he were amused by the situation.

The gentleman in the garden.

"Lady Christina," he said, bowing before coming toward her. "How good to meet you."

She could not say anything, half falling back into her seat as he came toward her. She saw the flicker of a frown on his brow, as he stared at her now in confusion as he drew near.

"You," she whispered, wrapping her arms around her middle in an attempt to keep herself calm. "It cannot be you."

He frowned, taking the seat opposite, leaning back and

crossing one leg over the other. "What do you mean, Lady Christina? Have we met before?"

For a moment, doubts assailed her. Perhaps she had been wrong to think that it was the same man. Perhaps, in the darkness of the gardens, she had made a mistake.

But if his crystal blue eyes were not memorable enough, his hands were. Her gaze fell to the bloodied, bruised knuckles he'd sustained from punching the other gentleman full in the face — and her whole world collapsed. She closed her eyes for a moment, willing the truth away.

"Lady Christina," Lord Ravenhall said again, frustration edging his words. "Whatever is the matter? This is not what I expected from our first meeting. My father assured me that you were a well-bred woman who was more than interested in becoming a future duchess."

A burst of anger forced her eyes open, and she saw her glare surprised him. She knew she should be upset that she was now betrothed to a violent man. She should be shocked at his behavior. But that was not what caused her blood to boil now.

"This is *not* our first meeting," she said, her voice shaking with a mixture of anger and upset. "Have you already forgotten how you kissed me in the gardens only an hour ago? Is it that you have been with so many women that one more was nothing to you? Or is it that I am so forgettable you hardly noticed me at all?"

She watched as his eyes widened, the irritation disappearing from his features almost at once. His skin paled, his blue eyes filling with shock.

"I am sorry, Lord Ravenhall, but there will be no courtship, no betrothal, no marriage," Christina continued, her arms slowly loosening about her waist as she drew in a few deep breaths. "I cannot commit my life to you, Lord Ravenhall, not after what I have seen."

He did not say anything for a long time, and Christina found she could not hold his stare any longer and turned her eyes away.

"I am afraid you must." His words were hard and sharp, piercing her very soul. "Your father will insist upon it."

She swallowed hard, knowing that he spoke the truth yet hoping desperately that, should she explain her reluctance to her father, he would allow her the opportunity to step back from the engagement.

"I can make up my own mind, Lord Ravenhall," she lied, turning back to face him as a strength she did not know she had begun to weave its way through her. "Our betrothal is not yet official, and I have no intention of making it so." She shook her head, her heart bursting with a sudden, fierce determination to protect herself. "I will not marry a gentleman such as you."

A small groan escaped him, and Christina glanced over to find him running one hand through his hair, sitting back in his chair and looking up at the ceiling. She felt no sympathy for him, her mind firmly fixed in her decision. He had brought this upon himself.

"Lady Christina, that was not the best first impression I could have made, I realize that," he said in a firm voice, and she snorted a bit at the understatement. "But what you saw — that is not the kind of gentleman I am. I do not go around threatening other gentlemen, nor kissing ladies without their consent."

"And I am to just believe this?" Christina exclaimed as he looked back at her steadily. She gave a skeptical laugh. "Words mean only so much, Lord Ravenhall. Actions tell all."

He got to his feet and paced the length of the room and back, stopping in front of her. "You know nothing of my situation, of what caused the quarrel between me and Lord

Northcliffe. Do not dare question my character, Lady Christina, when you know nothing at all about me."

"I know more than enough," she said, standing, her anger with him replacing any former nerves. "I believe I am beginning to understand why your father was so willing to have you marry the first woman who agreed to have you."

He swiftly turned toward her, and she thought, just for a moment, she caught a look of despair in his eyes before he quickly masked it with a narrowed glare.

"Watch your tone."

"We are not wed, my lord, and therefore, you have no cause to tell me how to behave," she said, crossing over to him and poking a finger into his chest. "And even if we *were* wed, I would not listen to you anyway."

"And now I am beginning to see why the daughter of a marquess has been on the shelf for so long."

Christina gasped at his words. Although she knew she had said something nearly the same to him, it did not lessen the bite of his words, for she knew there was truth in his statement. Before she could think of what she was doing, she reached back a hand and swung her arm toward his cheek, but he caught her wrist before she could connect.

"Now, now, Lady Christina, I thought you had an issue with violence?" He raised his eyebrows as he looked down at her

As angry as she was, she nonetheless couldn't miss the tremor that coursed through her body from where his hand held her wrist. He looked down at where they touched and he rubbed his thumb along the delicate bone of her wrist. Despite the fabric of her glove between their skin, she shivered and then cursed when she realized he had noticed as he looked up at her with a wicked grin.

* * *

DANIEL HAD WANTED to scare her. He needed his future bride to have no attachment to him, to want nothing more than an arrangement. He knew he had to marry in order to please his parents, keep his wealth, and continue his work, but he had no intention of marrying for anything more than continuing his name.

Then this woman had quite literally stumbled into his life.

She was right about one thing — he hadn't recognized her from the garden. He had been so hell-bent on taking his revenge on Lord Northcliffe he had hardly paid her any attention. He knew kissing a woman of the *ton* was a risk, but he had hoped the young woman hadn't been able to recognize him in the darkness, and wouldn't say anything in order to not bring any shame to herself.

Daniel had to admit it had been intoxicating to kiss her, to lose himself in a woman, just for a moment, as it had been so very long since he had. He could tell she was inexperienced, yet her passion had flared enough to incite him. It had been so dark in the gardens, she had been lost in the shadows the entire time, though now that he looked at his apparent future bride-to-be, he recognized the silvery dress, the lush curves he had felt under his hands. She certainly swelled in all the right places, and he was surprised to find that he had to tamp down his growing desire to pull her to him and feel her softness against him once more.

He gazed down at her now, realizing that the teasing of his lips was not simply contrived nor the remembrance of his training as a young lad. No, he was enjoying himself — and that scared him. His smile fell, and he let go of her wrist quickly, her eyes — a mysterious shade of gray — now clouded in confusion.

"Look here, Lady Christina, what you witnessed, what I did… there are circumstances surrounding my actions that you do not understand. I have demons from my past, and they are centered around the man you saw me with. I will not apologize, for I have nothing to be sorry for. You do not know the truth, although if you require it in order to follow through with this marriage, I will tell you all."

He saw her hesitate as her eyes searched his face. He took the opportunity to study her as well. He reached out toward her, noting her flinch slightly, but instead of grasping her shoulders and drawing her to him, he simply picked up the small dark blonde braid that had fallen and looped it back around her upswept hair. Her eyes widened, but she didn't move out of the way.

"Lord Hudson told me not to go after him, but I did not listen," he murmured, knowing she had no idea of what he spoke but continuing nonetheless. "I should have left him alone, but after what he did, I could not do anything but go." He shook his head, stepping back from her now as he pressed one hand firmly against the wall and looked away from her and down at the floor.

"Lord Ravenhall, I do not know what you are talking about, but it does not change my decision," Lady Christina replied, firmly. "Your demons are your own and are not an excuse for treating me so."

He turned to her then. She seemed a practical sort. Perhaps he was going about this all wrong. "Will you not allow me a chance to explain?" he said, slowly. "To show you that I am not the man you think?"

Christina frowned. "Why should you care what I think, Lord Ravenhall? If you do not marry me then I am certain there are plenty of other young ladies who will have you."

He could feel her eyes on him as he pushed himself away from the wall and returned to his chair. She was correct. Many women would be thrilled to marry a future duke, no matter how reclusive or horrible he was rumored to be. But he had no wish to court young women of the *ton*, and all would be made much easier for him if he continued with his parents' wishes. Besides that, he felt that a woman such as this one would not expect the romance a young, untried debutante might — romance that he had no time for.

"I have done you wrong, Lady Christina. I do not want my reputation to be sullied, not even in your eyes, for I cannot have any kind of shame brought to my family." He tried to remain calm and open, hoping to make her believe him. He opted for the truth. "Besides which, both of our parents wish for this match and I would not like to disappoint them. If you would but give me a chance to explain, to court you perhaps, then I am certain you might reconsider."

He could tell she was about to say no, to refuse him, but then she tilted her head back and studied him. He tried his best to remain earnest, to encourage her to believe in what he was saying, and give him one more chance.

"Very well, Lord Ravenhall," she finally said, slowly and softly. "I will allow you to court me, but nothing official is to be said until I have made up my mind. Will your parents agree to a bit of a delay?"

He felt relief wash over him, and some of the tension go out of his shoulders. Now it was a matter of not offending her too horribly.

"Yes, I am certain they will be persuaded to do just that," he said, getting to his feet and reaching for her hand. "Thank you, Lady Christina."

She gave him her gloved hand and he bowed over it. He wanted to bring it to his lips, to kiss her fingers, but he did not want to push things any further than they already were. He could see the confusion in her eyes, and he knew she was questioning her decision. Daniel would convince her that she was right in her choice. He had to.

CHAPTER 8

"*W*ell, Christina, I cannot say that I am pleased."

Drawing in a long, silent breath, Christina fixed her eyes on her father as he stood in their drawing room. She had known this moment was coming ever since she and Lord Ravenhall had exited the small room last evening with the news that they intended to court for a short time before making anything official. Lord Ravenhall had promised that a final decision would be reached within the week, which the Duke of Ware had reluctantly accepted. It seemed as though the duke had expected to make the announcement at the ball, but Lord Ravenhall had not backed down. At least that gave him some credibility in her eyes, although it was not enough to make her forget his actions in the gardens.

As Lord Ravenhall had spoken, Christina had seen the look in her father's eyes then — a look that told her he was not pleased with this decision. When he trained his gaze upon her, she knew he blamed her for the delay in the announcement.

Now she was determined to remain firm, although she

couldn't share all the details of what had occurred in the gardens with Lord Ravenhall. It was partly because she knew she shouldn't have been alone with him, but for some reason, she also felt that she had to protect him, though why that would be so, she had no idea.

"If you would let me explain, Father, I—"

"I cannot understand what the matter is," her father interrupted, blustering about, waving his hands theatrically. "Lord Ravenhall is a good and honest gentleman, who is one day to be a *duke*, and you are insisting that you must get to know him better before you agree to the betrothal?"

He looked at her as though she had gone raving mad but Christina held her ground, even though it appeared he would not allow her to offer any type of explanation. Perhaps that was for the best.

"Father, it was a mutual decision," she said, calmly, sitting before him, her hands folded in her lap. "Did you yourself not tell me that Lord Ravenhall would have to agree before it all went through? This is better than him outright rejecting the match, is it not?"

That took the wind out of his sails.

"Yes, I suppose," he muttered, taking his usual stance now, leaning on the mantelpiece. "But I'd presumed the duke had talked some sense into him. You do not have long to convince him that you will make a good wife. You are not the prettiest thing in the world, though you have a good head on your shoulders. Now that he's back in London, you do not want another young lady to catch his attention."

Ignoring the familiar sting of pain, Christina inclined her head. "I understand there is some urgency, Father, but I believe I must also determine whether he would make me a good husband," she said, refusing to bend. "It is only for a week and, should there be no agreement, then I am certain I can seek another gentleman's court soon enough."

For a moment, the vision of a wonderful Season floated in front of her eyes, the Season she had always hoped to have. Perhaps, if she chose to bring her engagement with Lord Ravenhall to a close, then there would be the chance to have that Season, filled with opportunity.

"If *this* Season does not end with you marrying the heir to the Duke of Ware, then it will be your cousin who takes you as his wife," her father grated, one hand thumping the top of the mantelpiece, startling her. "Do not think for one moment that I will allow you to make a stupid decision, Christina. To turn down a marquess, a future duke? I think not. It would be the height of embarrassment for our family!"

Horrified at the thought of marrying the one man who repulsed her more than any other, Christina stared at her father in shock. She knew that her cousin was a gambler, with very little money and the tiniest home to call his own since he had thrown the majority of his wealth away. She also knew that her father had no time or respect for the man, and she was shocked that he would even suggest such a thing.

"Father," she said, hoarsely, blood draining from her face. "You are not serious. You cannot stand Cousin George — would you really force me to marry a man like that?"

"I will do whatever I have to, to make sure you accept the Marquess of Ravenhall," he grated, his eyes narrowing as he turned to face Christina. "But this is entirely within your power, Christina. If the marquess does not accept you, then I will not force your cousin's hand into your own. However, if I find out that it is you who has turned from Lord Ravenhall, then I assure you that your marriage to Cousin George will be secured within the month." He stepped away from the mantelpiece, coming a little closer to her and, for the first time, Christina saw the anger burning in his eyes. "Do I make myself clear?"

Christina was frozen in place, not sure what to say or even how to respond, surprised at just how furious her father was. He always blustered about, to be sure, but he had never shown true anger like this toward her. Did he know that it had been her insistence that had stopped the engagement from being announced last evening?

"My lord?"

The butler stepped into the room, just as tears of frustration pooled in Christina's eyes. She blinked them away as the butler looked at them both apologetically, his hands held tightly in front of him. "I did knock, my lord, but there was no reply. Lord Ravenhall has come to call on Lady Christina."

"Of course," the marquess replied, grandly, as though everything was just as it should be. "Show him in at once."

The butler did as he was told, leaving Christina with only a few seconds to try to regain her composure. Her entire world shrank as she rose to greet Lord Ravenhall, as every door seemed to close around her. She was not to have the freedom to reject the engagement in the way she'd hoped. This discussion with her father had only made things all the worse.

She felt sick to her stomach.

"Ah, good afternoon Lord Ravenhall," her father said, as Christina dropped to a curtsy without raising her eyes to the man. "My daughter has very much been looking forward to seeing you again, but we had not thought it would be until this evening."

Lord Ravenhall smiled just as Christina managed to meet his gaze and, to her surprise, a wave of warmth crashed over her. With all that had occurred the evening prior, she had not taken the opportunity to fully admire just how handsome he was. He cut a dashing figure, and that bit of stubble still graced his cheeks. She wanted to run her hand over it, to see how it felt beneath her fingertips. She felt herself turning red as she thought of it, and suddenly she was aware of just how dowdy she must seem to him, particularly this morning. Christina was not exactly used to having callers. She had not made much of an effort with her hair, instructing her maid to tie it back in a simple chignon. Already she could feel pieces floating out of it — and not beautiful ringlets that would look fetching, but just limp, straight strands that fell to her shoulders. Her simple blue-gray day dress was one of her plainest, the muslin falling from a simple empire waist without any adornments. What with her red-rimmed eyes — which they must surely be given how they were stinging from lack of sleep — Christina was sure she made a less than pretty picture.

"I was hoping I might take your daughter out for a short walk around town, perhaps to the bookshop," Lord Raven-hall replied, seeming somewhat hopeful, and Christina narrowed her eyes at him, wondering what he was up to. "I hear you are very fond of reading, Lady Christina."

"I am," Christina managed to reply with some hesitation, as she wondered at this sudden transformation she saw in him.

His smile spread, though it didn't seem to reach his eyes, but he clapped his gloved hands together. "Capital! Then, what do you say, Lady Christina? A stroll?"

Christina looked at her father and saw him give her the smallest of nods, aware that she was expected to say yes instead of finding some kind of excuse.

"If you will just allow me to change," she replied, quietly, her stomach in turmoil, "then I will join you at the door presently."

* * *

THE WARMTH that Lord Ravenhall had shown toward Christina in the drawing room evaporated the moment they stepped outside, her maid following at a distance behind them. His smile vanished, his brow furrowed, and he did not so much as offer her his arm. Christina walked alongside him in silence, utterly wretched, knowing that at some point, she would have to make a decision as to whether she would accept the betrothal or risk that her father meant what he threatened. She wasn't entirely sure he would actually force her to marry George, or whether he was simply trying to make her do as he bid.

She couldn't exactly explain all of this to Lord Ravenhall, however. He would think her confused or lacking judgment. So instead, Christina stayed quiet on the matter. When he didn't say anything for some minutes, however, she could no longer take the silence stretching between them.

"Did you enjoy the remainder of the ball last evening?" Christina asked, tentatively.

He shrugged. "I did not stay long," he replied, not so much as looking at her. "I prefer to be at home."

"I see." There was nothing else to say and, to her frustration, they lapsed into silence once again. Christina was hit with a sudden vision of her future, a future of them living quietly and separately while pretending to all and sundry that they were as happy as could be.

She paused, her step slowing as her thoughts on the matter grew all the more. Was that such a terrible fate? Would it truly be a sad existence? To marry a man who would live his life as though she were not a part of it? It was, after all, the way she had lived with her father for so many years, and Christina had become quite adept at living in such a way as she knew many couples did as well. She had her books and, on occasion, her friends and perhaps, with Lord Ravenhall, there was the possibility of children. She could easily devote herself to them and not feel the loss of his companionship in any way, she thought. It would be less lonely than her current situation. The more Christina thought of having children of her own, someone to truly love and who would love her completely in return, the more she warmed to the idea.

"I suppose I should explain to you all that went on last evening."

Lord Ravenhall's baritone voice broke into her thoughts and, as she glanced up at him, saw that he was studying her with eyes that seemed to glitter like an aquamarine gemstone. A curl of anxiety rose in her stomach but she pushed it away, determined to remain strong.

"Yes, an explanation would be appreciated," she said, calmly, as they continued to walk together. "You were to explain to me exactly what it was that the man you attacked last evening had done to you to deserve such treatment."

Despite his grave countenance, she still believed it was likely to be something trivial, such as a card game, a stolen love or even horseflesh, but, then again, she could not forget the agony in his expression when he had spoken to her following the incident.

"Here," he said, turning the corner of the street and gesturing to the waiting carriage. "Please, climb in."

Christina paused suddenly in surprise, looking back at him. "I thought we were to stroll to the bookshop?"

"You need not be afraid," he replied, looking a little affronted. "I will not kidnap you or do anything untoward. This, however, cannot be spoken aloud, for fear that someone will overhear us. My friend, Lord Hudson, is within in order to confirm what it is I am to tell you."

Christina took a deep breath, set her shoulders, and made straight for the carriage, attempting to push her worry away. She nodded to her maid to wait atop for her. As Christina approached, she saw a gentleman lean out of the carriage door, a smile on his open, friendly face.

"And this must be Lady Christina," he exclaimed, stepping out of the carriage altogether. "It is my very great honor to meet you, my dear. Do come inside. Viscount Hudson at your service."

To her surprise, Christina liked the man at once. He was everything Lord Ravenhall was not. He was cleanly shaven with silky blond hair, wore a wide, welcoming smile, and looked at her with bright-green eyes that made her feel truly at home with him.

Without hesitation, she accepted his hand, smiled in return, and climbed inside.

CHAPTER 9

$\mathcal{D}$aniel couldn't help his relief that Lady Christina had accepted his offer to enter the carriage, glad that Hudson had been so willing to aid him in this task. While the entire garden ordeal had been a complete and utter disaster, at least she now allowed him the opportunity to explain himself.

Heat crept up his neck as he reflected on what he'd done thus far, fully aware of just how badly he'd lost his head when he'd seen Lord Northcliffe last evening. He could explain the situation, but he had still made the choice to act as he did. Daniel rapped on the roof of the carriage to tell his driver to move.

"Lady Christina," he began, sitting down next to Lord Hudson, leaning forward with his elbows on his knees. "The man you saw me with last night, the man I…"

"Attacked," Lady Christina said, crisply, her gray eyes fixed on his.

He cleared his throat, ignoring Hudson's grin at her forwardness.

"Yes, the one I attacked. His name is Lord Northcliffe, and he killed the woman I loved."

Lady Christina's face went white as he spoke, her hands clasping the sides of the seat.

"I was with Lord Ravenhall at the time, Lady Christina, and saw his reaction to Miss Churston's death," Hudson added, quietly. "I saw everything, except for the man who did it."

"Lord Northcliffe," Daniel continued, his voice growing hoarse as the memories assailed him once more. "was Laura's former gentleman. They had been courting for some time but she, I believe, broke off the attachment. He was enraged and continued to try and persuade her to allow their engagement to proceed, but she had met me." He swallowed hard, his head dropping so that he did not have to look into Lady Christina's wide eyes.

"Lord Northcliffe knew I intended to propose, for the news had gone all around White's by then. Laura came to my townhouse with her maid so that I might accompany her to a ball, where we would make the official announcement. However, I had been called away by an urgent message that stated my mother was desperately ill so I told my butler to seat Laura in the drawing room until I returned — or until Lord Hudson arrived as he was to accompany us for propriety's sake."

Closing his eyes, Daniel dragged in a shaking breath, rubbing his temples as though he could push away the memories. "When I realized that my mother was in full health and that the note had only been to take me away from my home, I returned there as quickly as I could, only to discover Laura lying on the threshold, blood pooling around her head." At Lady Christina's gasp, he glanced up to see her hands at her mouth. Hudson looked at him with some consternation, but Daniel needed her to understand the truth of what had happened, why he felt so strongly, and why he had done what he had. He shook his head, determined to get the last few words out. "She had been bludgeoned. She died."

There came a few moments of complete silence. Daniel forced himself to remain calm, to focus on his breathing so that his memories could not take hold. Most likely he would have nightmares this evening, but for now, he simply needed to keep his anger at bay.

"The butler was certain it was Lord Northcliffe," Hudson said as Daniel sat up straighter, forcing himself to look at Lady Christina. "But the authorities could not arrest a gentleman — a viscount at that — on what one dazed butler said, even though it makes sense to believe it was him."

"My goodness," Lady Christina whispered, her hands dropping to her lap. "I am so sorry, Lord Ravenhall. I had no idea."

"No," Daniel replied heavily. "How could you?"

She tilted her head and studied him then, and Daniel was struck, just as he had been last evening, by just how intense her eyes were. They were an unusual shade of gray with just a touch of blue behind them, but there was compassion woven into her gaze. While he knew none would ever describe her as a great beauty, there was a gentle grace about her that drew him in.

Not that he could ever feel anything more than friendship with a woman, not after Laura.

"And can I ask why you are interested in marrying me, Lord Ravenhall?" Lady Christina asked, softly. "It appears as though you are still caught up in a swirl of emotions over your former love and Lord Northcliffe."

Daniel swallowed the ache in his throat and tried his best to explain, choosing not to keep anything back from her. He had entirely forgotten about Hudson's presence and instead spoke directly to her.

"Because I have no choice. My father, the duke, is unaware as to how I spend my time. As far as he is concerned, I have become a bit of a social recluse, and I suppose that is true." He spread his hands, shrugging. "I want justice, Lady Christina. I want justice for Laura and for those who cannot speak for themselves. Therefore, I allow Lord Hudson and others to go about London and help those in need. On occasion, I come to town to involve myself when and where I must, but for the most part, I remain in the country, ensuring that my estate and my tenants are all well looked after."

Lady Christina frowned, and for a moment, Daniel wondered if she was about to exclaim over just how ungentlemanly it was to involve oneself with those in the lower classes, but to his surprise, she did not.

"And might I ask why this requires you to be married?" she asked, slowly. "Can you not continue with this work without a wife?"

He shook his head. "My father still has control over my fortune and my accounts. If I do not do as he orders, then the money will disappear entirely until I follow through on his wishes. He wants an heir to the family line."

Watching Lady Christina, he noted the way her cheeks reddened, her eyes darting away from him, and for a moment, Daniel caught himself wondering what it would be like to have her in his bed. A prickle of desire climbed through his limbs. He remembered her mouth under his, the passion he had felt hiding within her. What would it be like to explore that further?

He pushed away the fleeting thought, focusing instead on the practicalities of the situation they found themselves in.

"Then it appears we are in much the same position," Lady Christina replied, eventually, her lips curving down as she continued to look away from him. "My father insists I marry my brute of a cousin if I turn away from our engagement, Lord Ravenhall. I had no intention of so easily accepting our match, but it is beginning to appear I have less of a choice than I thought."

Anger pooled in his stomach anew, but on her behalf this time. He felt for her in this, as he knew what it was like to have a father force one into such a situation. He studied her closely, now. Her mouth was set in a firm line and while she didn't seem particularly pleased at the prospect of marrying him, she certainly seemed more amenable to it today than she had the night before.

He sighed. "I cannot promise you a life of gaiety, Lady Christina. I fully intend to return to my country estate, once I have brought about what I have planned for Lord Northcliffe."

"And what is that?" Lady Christina asked, her voice void of emotion. "You wish to do to him what he did to your first love?"

There was no censure in her voice, no horror in her eyes or shudder of her lips as she spoke. Daniel looked at her steadily and, instead, saw something like sympathy, or compassion, emerging in her expression.

"I suppose that it would be a lie not to admit that," he said, quietly. "Yes, I do wish for his demise. How that will come about, I am unsure. I do not wish to bring scandal to my family, but Lord Northcliffe must be made to pay for what he did."

Lady Christina nodded slowly, and Daniel wanted to reach out and brush back the silky strands of hair that had come loose and floated around her shoulders.

"I understand your need for revenge, Lord Ravenhall, but I may take issue with the way in which you propose to go about it," she said, and he sighed. She said she understood, but she couldn't, not truly. "You say you know Lord Northcliffe to be the culprit, but in truth, it seems you do not with absolute certainty. If you are fighting for justice, then you must know that you cannot take the life of a man not proven guilty."

She fixed him with her gaze and Hudson abruptly sat up straighter in self-satisfaction, as it seemed he and Lady Christina were of like minds on the matter.

"I must ask you, before you do anything you will regret, to assure yourself that you are correct in your assumptions and," her voice became much softer now, "please, at least consider approaching this in another way."

He looked at her, their gazes meeting, and he gave a short, jerky nod, not wanting to agree but knowing that if this was the only thing she asked of him, he couldn't refuse her. She surprised him when she broke their gaze and turned to his friend. "Lord Hudson," she said. "Might you give me a few minutes alone with Lord Ravenhall?"

Hudson seemed momentarily surprised, but gifted her with one of his wide, charming smiles, and Lady Christina returned it with a small smile of her own. Daniel felt the taste of bitterness in his mouth, and he wondered at his reaction. He didn't care what Christina thought of other men. She was simply a means to an end.

Daniel rapped on the roof to stop the carriage, and then waited as his friend disembarked before turning toward Lady Christina. What was it she wished to say? Looking back at her, he saw her turn her smile toward him as Lord Hudson closed the door and his heart jumped within him until he saw the corners of her mouth straighten once more.

No. He could not feel this. He could not allow himself to feel anything for the lady opposite him. It would be a betrayal of Laura, a forgetting of all that they'd shared. And it would be opening himself up to the possibility of feeling that pain once more, a pain that he refused to ever entertain again. No, no matter what happened, he would remain aloof and distant, never seeking to grow closer to her, pushing her away in turn. His heart would never be given to another again.

"Lord Ravenhall, may I speak plainly?" Lady Christina asked, sitting back in her seat and pinning him with her direct gaze. "There has been so much happening between us in the last few hours that I am struggling to think clearly, and perhaps it would be better to share what is on my mind."

Daniel nodded, a little taken aback at her frankness. This was nothing like Laura, who had been quiet and genteel, never truly giving voice to her thoughts unless he asked her directly.

"My father is forcing my hand, as is yours," Lady Christina began, a wry smile on her face that made his lips turn up slightly in response. "Therefore, I suggest that we move forward with our engagement and set a wedding date."

Daniel was surprised at her sudden agreement, but nodded all the same. "Yes, it is rather inevitable. I am glad you agree."

"It will save me from my detestable cousin and ensure that you can continue doing as you please," Lady Christina said, as though they were conducting a business transaction — which, he supposed, they were. "I realize that you are still in love with another woman, despite the fact she is gone from us," she continued softly. "I do not intend to compete with her, though I do ask that, perhaps, you and I can be friends with one another. I should not like to be completely alone."

He frowned, wondering at this. "I will eventually remove to the country, and I have much with which to occupy my time."

She gave a slight shrug. "I have lived in the country at my father's estate for a long time, Lord Ravenhall. I find more than enough to do without growing desperate for his continuous company."

He arched one eyebrow as he stared back at her, becoming aware of what she was saying. She did not need him to be happy and content, even though — to his surprise — he began to realize that he wouldn't mind so much if she preferred to spend more time with him. Perhaps some company might be nice for a change.

"Very well," he agreed, slowly, shocked that his heart was filled with a sudden, unexpected hope that, perhaps, this marriage would not be as difficult as he had once thought. "We shall, of course, have to consummate the marriage. My father is correct in stating that I will need to produce an heir."

Lady Christina did not flinch nor look away, but her cheeks turned such a warm red that Daniel was almost inclined to laugh. His amusement died, however, as he realized just how lovely she appeared to be in that moment, even though her coloring was vastly different from that of Laura's.

But you can barely remember what Laura looked like.

The small voice in his head threw guilt directly in his face, making him suck in a breath as Lady Christina cleared her throat quietly. This could not happen. He had to stop thinking of Lady Christina, had to stop remembering how he'd kissed her last evening and just how much he'd enjoyed it. He had to keep her close enough to ensure they were married, and then he would put as much distance between them as possible.

"Perhaps we should tell our parents the good news at this evening's dinner," he suggested after clearing his throat, and he gestured for Hudson to return to the carriage. "The first banns can be called a week on Sunday."

Lady Christina nodded, her hands tightening in her lap as

she looked away from him. "Thank you, Lord Ravenhall. This marriage shall be good for both of us, I am sure."

"I certainly hope so, Lady Christina," Daniel murmured, as Hudson climbed back inside, a hopeful look on his face. "Well, Hudson, it appears as though I am to be a married man after all."

"Then may I be the first to offer you my congratulations," Lord Hudson exclaimed, clapping his hands as he beamed at them both. "Wonderful news."

"Thank you, Lord Hudson," Lady Christina murmured. "You are very kind."

He chuckled, as Daniel's gaze drifted out of the window. He no longer felt the tingle of jealousy, not when he knew now that Lady Christina was to be his.

"Not at all, Lady Christina," Hudson continued, and Daniel reminded himself that charm was simply part of Hudson's demeanour. "I just hope there is an engagement ball so that I might have my own opportunity to meet an eligible young lady! Perhaps matrimony is in my future after all."

"Perhaps it is," Daniel agreed, folding his arms across his chest and opening the carriage door to help Lady Christina down to return her home. "Who knows, Hudson? Mayhap it will sneak up on you, just as it has done on me." Shooting a glance toward Lady Christina, he noted her frown as she looked out the door, not turning her head back toward him. He remembered he must keep her happy. "But, then again, perhaps that is not altogether a bad thing."

Lady Christina smiled.

CHAPTER 10

*C*hristina was not entirely sure who was happier about their marriage agreement — her father or Lord Ravenhall's parents. While Christina questioned Lord Ravenhall's motives, she now had no doubts that the Duke and Duchess of Ware simply wanted him to be happy — and to begin to produce heirs. The month between their announced betrothal and the wedding flew by. While Christina's father had primarily been concerned about the engagement actually occurring, the Duchess of Ware was more than pleased to step in and help make all of the arrangements.

She accompanied Christina to a dress fitting, as did Lord Ravenhall's youngest sister, Polly, who was as exuberant as she had been at the theatre. It was somewhat disconcerting to be measured and fitted next to a woman so beautifully shaped, but Polly was so busy describing how perfect Christina's wedding would be that it didn't seem she was paying any attention to Christina's figure — that was, until she saw her in her dress.

"Oh, my," she breathed, as she came to stand beside

Christina, placing two hands on her arm as she continued to look at her reflection with her eyes open wide. "You are absolutely beautiful, Christina."

Christina wasn't sure about that, but she did know it was the most extravagant dress she had ever worn. The creamy bodice was lacy, the material extending to the puffed cap sleeves with their gathered trim. The belt that wrapped just under her bosom was a band of intricate braids, and flowing from it was a long, straight skirt inlaid with an embroidered floral pattern, which fanned out at the bottom of the dress and extended through the train behind her. Christina was already shaking her head before Polly finished speaking.

"I cannot wear this," she said.

"Why ever not?" the Duchess of Ware asked, coming to stand with them.

"It is just so... extravagant," she responded. "I'm not sure where I shall ever be able to wear it again following our wedding, as Lord Ravenhall seems very intent on returning to the country right away. It would be better to have a dress that I can wear for many different occasions."

"Oh, come now," Polly said, waving away her concern. "Are you forgetting that you are to be the wife of a marquess, and one day a duchess? Daniel can spare the expense."

"Yes, but—"

"It is already nearly finished and looks altogether perfect," the duchess said, smiling and bringing a hand to her arm. "There is nothing to be done now."

So here she stood on her father's arm at the back of the church, wearing the elegant dress as she looked down the long aisle of St. George's to where Lord Ravenhall stood waiting for her. The pews were nearly empty, save his rather large and growing family along with Lord Hudson, her father, Lady Aster, her brother and his wife, and Lady Beatrice and her family.

85

Christina fixed a smile to her face and clutched the bouquet of peonies — her favorite — and other greenery. Christina wasn't sure why she needed the flowers in hand, but Polly had insisted. In fact, Polly and her mother had planned nearly the whole thing, after declaring that Christina was being much too practical for a wedding that should be as romantic as possible. Polly had even sat at Christina's side as she prepared herself that morning, instructing Christina's maid on just how to thread the wreath of flowers through her hair.

Christina set her jaw and began walking toward Daniel. She had hardly seen him in the past weeks, and when she had, there were always family members present so they had never been alone. She didn't know why she cared, though she realized that a part of her still held out hope that her husband could come to feel some affection or desire for her.

Her eyes met his, and she found she couldn't turn her head away from his crystal-blue stare. He looked… resigned, and her heart seemed to shrink a bit in disappointment while she felt the bitter smile come to her face. He was dressed in black as if attending a funeral. His jacket, so perfectly tailored to his figure, opened to show his equally dark waist-coat over his black knee breeches and stockings. The only brightness to be seen was the white silk cravat tied around his neck. She swallowed and broke her eyes away from his when they neared.

"I'm proud of you, my girl," her father whispered to her, to which she turned her head away. Finally, he was proud of her, and for something that required nothing on her part but obeying. The rest of the ceremony passed in a blur, and it was over so quickly she nearly didn't realize when it was finished.

Daniel took her arm without a word, and as he walked her out of the church to the carriage waiting to convey them to his father's home for the wedding breakfast, all she could think was, *what have I done?*

* * *

SHE WAS BREATHTAKING.

He could never have imagined it before, would never have thought that the plain but pretty, curvy woman could ever be described as beautiful, but when she had stepped into the church, the sun seemed to shine perfectly through the stained glass window reflecting upon the creamy white of her dress. When Daniel had looked back behind him at the painting of Jesus and his disciples staring down at him, somehow he was filled with a sense of peace that he was doing the right thing. When he returned his gaze to her, she seemed somewhat ethereal walking toward him, and he would have thought her an angel were it not for the glimmer of a hesitation in her gray eyes.

He shook hands with her father, and then stood there, staring at her, but her eyes seemed far away, and an ache within him longed to convince her to stay here, with him, to more truly agree to the words spoken between them. But alas, it was not to be. For to open himself up again could mean the end of him, and he could never feel that pain again.

When he took her on his arm to leave the church, he spoke not a word, but led her out the doors, into his carriage, and traveled the short distance to his parents' home.

At Christina's swift intake of breath, he turned to look at her. "Are you all right?" he asked, to which he nodded.

"Of course," she replied, never one to allow emotion to overcome her, something he appreciated about her. "I have seen the home of the duke and duchess many times, of course, but never did I think I would be entering — and entering as family."

As they exited the carriage, he looked up at the impressive manor and tried to see if from the eyes of someone else for the first time. It wasn't altogether elaborately built, but it was certainly impressive, the tall brick building with its many well-ordered windows.

"Come along, then," he said, and helped her down and through the front doors. In his rush out of the church, they had arrived before many of his family members, although the servants were there to greet him, his own butler at the ready to help where he was needed.

"My lord," Woodward said, approaching him and taking his hat. "May I be one of the first to wish you congratulations on your nuptials. I am certain that you and Lady Ravenhall will have a long and splendid future together."

"Thank you, Woodward," he said, turning away from the man and continuing down the hallway, rapidly making his way toward the dining room.

"Lord Ravenhall," he heard from behind him, and he turned to see with some surprise that Christina was rushing down the hallway to keep up with him. He slowed his strides slightly so she could catch up. "Lord Ravenhall, the butler seemed rather— my goodness!"

* * *

It took entering the family's home for Christina to finally realize the significance of marrying into the family of a duke.

She stood, staring wide-eyed at the dining hall. Though it would primarily be their families in attendance, the side table was near to bursting with food — omelets, bacon, sliced ham, haddock, fruits, and bread and rolls with various jams and marmalade spread out before them. In the middle of the table stood one of the largest wedding cakes she had ever seen, though she had to admit she had hardly any occasion to see wedding cake in her past. How many people was it supposed to feed?

"Who is attending this breakfast?" she asked, looking at Daniel, and he shrugged and laughed slightly. "My family and yours. My mother has... a propensity for the extreme."

Before she could respond, the woman in question came sailing into the room, dressed in a beautiful gown of violet, ostrich plumes extending out the back.

"Welcome!" she said, coming over and kissing Christina on the cheek, startling her. "Ah, how lovely it will be to have nearly all of our families together. It has been so long, and now, finally, my children have all found someone with whom to share their life. Oh, I do not think I have ever been happier. I can hardly wait until your children arrive."

"*My* children?" Christina asked, confused. Whose children did the duchess mean would be attending?

"Yes, your children, whenever the time should come for them — hopefully soon," said the duchess with a twinkle in her eye, those eyes that were so similar to Daniel's, and Christina's cheeks grew hot. Oh. She wasn't sure she had ever heard a duchess speak of such things, but then, the Harrington family was proving to be somewhat unconventional.

Soon the room was filled with all of them, and Christina did her very best to remember the names of them all as they were presented to her. They were introduced by title and by given name, and she tried to recall which ones were the couples. The next eldest, Thomas, had arrived with his wife Eleanor and their two daughters. Christina was startled by the tan of their skin and the blonde of their hair, very clearly kissed by the sun. She was told they lived at sea much of the time, and she was rather confused, but before she could question them any further, she was introduced to Daniel's elegant sister Violet, her hair a few shades darker than

Daniel's, so in contrast to Polly's blonde locks. Polly's husband, Lord Taylor, and Violet's husband, Lord Greville, seemed to be particularly close friends, and she was briefly introduced to Violet's infant before he was taken upstairs to a nursery. Finally, Daniel's youngest brother, Benjamin, arrived with a small, shy woman on his arm who was introduced to her as Sophie. Christina shared a smile with her, sensing that they would forge a bond as newcomers to this large, abundant family.

She felt overwhelmed when she finally sat down but found she merely had to sit quietly and listen, such was the merriment of the siblings upon seeing one another. They talked over one another, despite Marie's admonishment to be polite and silent, and Christina smiled as she could see what they must have been like as children. Only Daniel sat stoically beside her, saying nothing as he sipped his coffee, though she could see a warmth in his eyes that she hadn't before.

"Tell me, Christina, how long will you remain in London?" asked Polly from across the table, to which Christina looked to Daniel, though he simply shrugged.

"I — I am not entirely sure," she answered, "though I do love the countryside, so I will be equally happy wherever we go."

"I understand your sentiments," Polly agreed. "I, too, have come to love life outside of London, though we often find ourselves here. Do you ride?"

"I do," she responded. "I spent much of my youth at my father's country home."

"It is too bad, then, that Daniel is not much of a horseman," Polly said with a wink, to which Daniel finally spoke up.

"I think that is quite enough, Polly," he said firmly.

"I was only teasing, Daniel," she said with a laugh. "Do

you remember when I was young and learning to ride? You said you would teach me, but then we came to the fence and we met that young woman. You were so captivated, you completely abandoned me, and instead—"

"I said *enough*, Polly!" Daniel exclaimed, bringing his fist down on the table, and the room went silent as all of the faces of their guests and family turned to stare at him.

"Perhaps we should go," Christina said quietly, her heart hammering despite the calm outer facade she tried to maintain. Daniel simply nodded, stood, and walked out of the room, practically leaving her behind.

"Thank you so much, your graces," she said, curtsying to the duke and duchess before hurrying out of the room after the surly, angry man, who she now called her husband.

CHAPTER 11

"*L*ord Ravenhall!" Christina called from behind him, but Daniel ignored her as he picked up his hat from Woodward, who was waiting for him, ever faithfully, at the door and continued outside. For once he was thankful that his townhouse was but across the street from that of his parents, which meant that he wouldn't have to walk far among the prying eyes of society.

His foot hit the bottom step when he heard his name once more — only this time, it was not a shout, but rather said in a steady, calm, yet commanding tone that unnerved him.

"Daniel Harrington, you will stop walking this instant and wait for your wife. I will not race after you like a dog on your heels."

He turned to look at her and nearly laughed, he was so shocked at her words. She stood with her fists at her hips, looking down at him over her pert nose which she held high in the air. She reminded him of a nursemaid chastising a child. He opened his mouth, but, realizing there was nothing he could say to her to properly explain why he was running, he turned back and took a step down the road.

She sailed down the stairs behind him, however, and when he looked up he saw open-mouthed faces of passersby and realized he had to stop and wait for her, as it seemed she had no issue with causing a scene in the middle of Mayfair. His mother would never forgive him.

"We can speak out here, or we can go inside and have our discussion in private," she said low in his ear once she had reached him. "It's your choice."

He looked at her with a glower that had served to scare most away from him over the years, but she simply arched an eyebrow and began striding down the street, until it was he that had to rush to keep up with her.

"You do realize how you are speaking to the Marquess of Ravenhall, future Duke of Ware?" he asked her wryly as they neared his house, not nearly as impressive as the Ware manor, but striking nonetheless.

"And *you* do realize that as of this morning, I am the Marchioness of Ravenhall, future Duchess of Ware?" she retorted, and he nearly smiled in spite of himself. "Do not try to scare me, Daniel. It will never work."

"Daniel, is it?"

She nodded curtly. "We are married now, and it is a lovely name. Someone may as well use it."

He allowed her to enter his home — their home — before him, and somehow Woodward was there with them, apparently having followed them down the street.

"Welcome home, my lord, my lady," he said with a bow, and Christina wandered through the entrance and down the corridor, looking into each room as she went, slowly peeling off her gloves.

"It looks as though it has had a lady's touch," she said, looking at Daniel quizzically.

"My mother," he offered by way of explanation.

"Did you not care to choose your own furnishings?" she

asked when she walked into the drawing room, and he noted her eyeing the overstuffed upholstery and floral decor. She didn't seem the flowery sort of woman.

He shrugged again. "I did not expect to be in London long," he said. "Only long enough to dissuade my father from whatever reason he had brought me here."

"Ah," she said. "To avoid me, you mean."

"At the time, I did not know the full extent of his plans, though I had a feeling he was going to encourage me toward matrimony. As it happens, we will be leaving in due time, anyway."

"Once you find Lord Northcliffe."

"Once I find Lord Northcliffe."

They faced one another until he felt uncomfortable by her pointed stare, which seemed to reach into the depths of his soul and read all he felt there.

"What is it you wish to say?" he finally asked, leading her to the sitting area of the room, where she chose the small settee.

"I would like to know why, when your sister began to reminisce, you flew out of the house as if you were being hunted, with that look of despair in your eyes. I know it was not her teasing that bothered you, but the story she told. I am assuming the young woman she mentioned was your Miss Churston?"

Daniel had no desire to sit here and discuss this with her, but she had a point — as his wife, if nothing else, he owed her an explanation.

"It was."

"Daniel, I…" She paused and looked down at her hands, clenched tightly together in her lap, and he realized she perhaps wasn't quite as composed as she outwardly presented herself. "What happened to Miss Churston — and to you — is unfathomable. Perhaps, however, instead of continuing this quest for vengeance, you would be better served to let go of your past, and remember her for who she was, not what happened to her. It's the only way you will be able to move on with your life."

He heard her words — he did — and deep down inside of him, he realized the truth in them. But not finding justice for Laura? As he had held her in his arms, he had promised her that he would find whoever killed her and make him pay for what he did. He was so close now, to not follow through on his vow was incomprehensible. How could Christina even think of suggesting such a thing?

The familiar fury that rose inside of him was almost a relief, for it was an emotion that he well recognized, that he knew what to do with. He said nothing for a moment as he stood, looking down at Christina, wearing what he knew to be a sneer on his face. She had said she wasn't afraid of him, but now looking at her, at the way her eyes widened, he could tell that she was rethinking her words.

"Who do you think you are?" he asked, hearing his words come out in a growl. "You think because we have been married for what, an hour, you can question everything I stand for, try to make me forget the woman I love? I will remind you, *my lady*, that I did not marry you because I felt anything for you. No, I married you so that I could hold onto my wealth, the wealth that allows me to continue to fight for what I believe in, for the people who have lost either those they love or any hope to find anything good in this world. Have you ever lost someone you love? Have you ever found yourself with nowhere to turn, no one to help you in your time of need? I gather not. You are the privileged daughter of a marquess, who has spent her life in a stately London manor or an extravagant country home, with her every necessity looked after. You need not concern yourself with my thoughts or activities any longer, Lady Ravenhall. Keep to your own pastimes, and I will keep to mine."

Her eyes had widened as he spoke, and now he could hardly see her gray irises through the sheen of tears that covered them. She had backbone, however, he would give her that. Most women would run cowering from him, but she did not. Instead, she stood and walked over to him until they were nearly toe-to-toe. She was of average height for a woman, and he still towered over her, but she had a silent power within her that kept him from dwarfing her.

"Very well, Lord Ravenhall," she said, her voice calm and serene, but for a slight crack that he nearly missed. "Do what you wish. Just know that I had no thought but for your own welfare. I take back that concern."

She began walking to the door, before turning around to make one last remark.

"And Ravenhall? Assume what you want, but you know nothing about me. Nothing."

* * *

As soon as she was out of her husband's sight, Christina turned and fled down the corridor. She had never been in the house before — her house now — but she ran up the stairs as fast as her voluminous skirts would allow her, and found herself in a hall of doors. The second on the left opened easily, and she stepped inside an elegantly decorated bedchamber. It was apparently a guest room, for no personal items could be seen, but she welcomed the anonymity of the room that should allow her some privacy.

Christina shut the door behind her and leaned back against it, all of the strength that had sustained her to make it thus far without losing her composure suddenly drained. The tears that had threatened since Daniel had made his accusations against her began to fall down her cheeks, and as she sank down to the floor amidst the folds of her gown, she began to weep. She realized the utter foolishness of what she had done, and what she had hoped for without hardly realizing it herself.

When she'd agreed to marry Daniel, she had known there would be no love between them, nothing beyond friendship and a partnership. They had married to avoid the alternatives threatened to them by their respective parents. And yet... deep down within her, she had hoped for more. While she knew his heart was still with his dead fiancée, she had hoped that perhaps he could, at the very least, come to care for her. She had thought that perhaps he desired her, but it seemed that, too, was fiction created by her imagination, something she had held out hope for but could simply never be.

No, it was worse than that. For rather than simply ignore her, he had spoken to her words that had cut her to the core. She thought back to the first time they had talked, when he had told her that now he understood why she was unmarried. It seemed her father was right. Her bluestocking ways, her practicality, her penchant for saying what needed to be said in order to come to the reality of the situation — it was more than a man could handle in a wife.

She allowed herself this moment of weakness, this sorrow at her situation and what the rest of her life was going to apparently become. She wasn't sure how long she sat there with tears falling down her face until finally she stood up, wiped her face on her beautiful white gloves as she could find nothing else, and looked bleakly around her. This was her home now. This was her life. And she wasn't going to let a man who refused to allow her entry into his heart or soul to darken the rest of her days. She would find her own happiness. With new resolve, she set her shoulders, wrenched open the door, and marched out to face whatever was waiting for her.

CHAPTER 12

*H*e never returned.

Christina had spent the rest of the day acquainting herself with her new home. Despite the fact that Daniel had told her he meant to be away from here as soon as possible, she knew that in all likelihood they would require a London residence. She could tell the house had been decorated rather quickly, and there were some changes she would like to make, but they could wait for another day.

More importantly, she tried to become better acquainted with the staff who greeted her. Besides the butler and the valet, most were newly hired and therefore had no allegiance to Daniel nor to the family. It was up to her to ensure they were properly treated and trained. Having run her family's home in the country for years now, she had no problem with this, and she set about things quickly. Her lady's maid had accompanied her, thankfully, which meant that Christina needn't bother herself with unpacking her own essentials, and before long she was satisfied that all was in order.

She changed from her beautiful gown into a blue day dress that was much more comfortable. She vowed she would find an occasion to wear the fine, expensive dress once again — hopefully at an event that proved to be much happier than the one she'd worn it at this morning.

The manor wasn't particularly ornate, which suited her. The aesthetics were lovely, of course, but what was more important was that the home flowed — that there was an ease in which the servants could move from one room to another, from the kitchen to the dining room without the food becoming cold, and that it wasn't far for guests to travel from dinner to the drawing room.

For that, Christina applauded the architect of the home.

While she was pleased when she had found things to be in order, the lingering unease in the pit of her stomach remained. She wondered when she would see Daniel, whether he would have cooled some from their heated exchange. Would he apologize? Would he realize she was only trying to help him live a life that had some brightness, some joy?

And tonight — would he come to her bed? As much as she dreaded seeing him again and was nervous about the marriage act, when she thought of their previous kiss, of the time they had touched before... a tingle of desire coursed through her, one she cursed as a betrayal of her body. She should hate Daniel for what he'd said to her, and yet she had seen moments of who he was, who he had been underneath the layers of pain, vengeance, and anger that he had cloaked himself with in order to keep everyone out. She wanted to peel back those layers, to find the man underneath.

Daniel had not appeared at supper. His butler told her he had gone out, for what reason he'd never revealed. She tried not to think of where her husband might have been. She hoped it was to do the work he told her of and refused to think he might be at a gentlemen's club or some other estab-lishment. She didn't begrudge his time away — she only wished he would share with her what he was doing, for perhaps she could help in some way. His work seemed valuable, though she questioned some of his methods.

Well, she thought as she prepared for bed, he had to come home at some point, and she assumed he would want his wedding night, to consummate this marriage. If nothing else, he had certainly expressed his desire for an heir. She had changed into her practical nightgown, had sat on the edge of the bed and waited for him.

Until eventually she grew too tired, and climbed underneath the covers of her new bed, finally falling into a fitful sleep.

* * *

DANIEL FINISHED his tour of the house that Hudson had found, the one that was to shelter additional women and children who needed his help. Satisfied, he turned on his heel and exited, his friend following close behind.

"Ravenhall," Hudson began, but before he could say anything, Daniel raised his hand.

"Do not say what I think you are going to say, Hudson," he said, fixing a scowl on his friend before continuing down the stairs.

"Why, because you know very well yourself where you ought to be at this moment?" Hudson asked, his eyebrows raised. "You have a very lovely bride waiting for you at home on your *wedding* night, and here you are, with me, in an abandoned house. I'm not sure what that says about you, Ravenhall, but I do question your choice."

Daniel gave a slight growl before hauling himself up into his coach. "Never fear, Hudson, I am returning home now."

"And what was that earlier at the wedding breakfast? Why, you stormed out of there so fast I thought your coat was on fire. I feared your mother was going to have an apoplexy. It is not as though we expect impeccable social graces from you any longer, but I had thought at the very least you would have more respect for your mother and fath—"

"I said enough!" Daniel ground out, but Hudson was not affected. He simply shook his head at him, further angering Daniel.

"I know there is nothing you will do to me, Ravenhall," he said. "You are angry only because I speak the truth — a truth that you know well inside you, although you are loathe to admit it. Is this how your Miss Churston would have wanted you to live the rest of your life?"

Daniel was silent for a moment as he contemplated Hudson's question. The truth was, he wasn't entirely sure how Laura Churston would want him to live his life. He had thought he loved her, and he was attracted to her sweet beauty, her quiet charm, and her grace, but as Christina and now Hudson were questioning him all the more about his past, he was beginning to realize that he hadn't actually known her quite as well as he thought he had.

It was part of the reason why he'd stormed out following Polly's storytelling, why he had become so very angry with Christina. The feelings he had thought for so long he felt for Laura were beginning to fade. The anger and hatred had consumed him so that he had forgotten what it felt like to be happy. And to let go of that, to forget her, made him feel like he was tarnishing her memory, was doing nothing to avenge her death, a death that he, indirectly, had caused.

"I don't know Hudson," he finally said. "I just do not know."

After bidding farewell to Hudson and entering his own home, Daniel slowly walked down the corridor and stopped in front of what he knew to be Christina's room. He paused for a moment outside the door, raising his hand — whether to knock or open it, he wasn't sure — but he stopped himself. He couldn't go to her, not like this. It wasn't fair to her, nor to himself. So instead, he continued down the hall, entered his rooms, poured a brandy, and sat there in silence, staring at the flames that licked at the grate in front of him.

CHAPTER 13

ONE MONTH LATER

"*D*aniel?"

Daniel held his breath as Christina walked into the study, for he found her presence to suddenly overwhelm the room.

"Yes?" he murmured, shuffling about some papers on his desk as he tried to ignore the way his heart had quickened its pace. "Is something wrong, Lady Ravenhall?"

There was a short pause. "No, Daniel, there is nothing wrong. I was just wondering if, perhaps, you would wish to walk with me this afternoon?"

Daniel shook his head firmly. The last thing he wanted was to be out with his wife so that all of society could see them. It had been a month since they had been married, a month which involved them basically ignoring one another. They often had supper together or occupied the same room, but they spoke primarily out of politeness. He knew this was of his own doing. He had said things to her that were unpardonable, for which he didn't know how to go about asking her forgiveness. For while he knew he had been in error, he also knew that he was not going to change his mind. He would continue his work, continue his search for North-cliffe. If he did not, he didn't think he could live with himself.

"No, I do not have time for a walk today," he said, not looking at her. "I have a great deal of business to attend to."

She did not say anything for a moment, and Daniel wondered whether or not she was about to grow angry with him, but instead of becoming upset, she simply sighed. Her eyes met his as he raised them but he looked away at once, hating the sadness written in her expression. It was not his fault that she was so lonely. This was, after all, what they had agreed to. And yet... her quiet presence, her practical manner, the way in which she seemed to make everything flow so effortlessly around her, drew him to her in a way he couldn't entirely explain.

"Might I inquire what it is you are doing?" Christina asked softly, coming a little closer to his desk, and the fresh, clean scent of the lavender soap she used swirl about him. "Is it about Lord Northcliffe?"

Daniel sat back in his chair, looking up at her, trying not to be affected at her nearness. "No, it is not about Lord Northcliffe. I have not seen the man for some time which perhaps means he has left London."

"But you intend to pursue him regardless?"

A wave of irritation crashed over him as he saw the questions in her eyes. This had nothing to do with his wife, even though she clearly wanted to be involved. This was his battle, his revenge to take. It was best that she kept to herself and left him to do whatever it was he intended.

"Lady Ravenhall, please allow me to work things out for myself, as regards Lord Northcliffe," he said firmly, ignoring the way she frowned as he spoke, at the disappointment that flashed in her eyes. "This is not a matter with which you need to concern yourself."

"You are my husband now, Daniel," she replied, her lips thinning, as clearly, her patience was beginning to wane. "I have every right to ask you what it is you are doing and to offer you my aid."

"And I have every right to refuse it, as I always will," Daniel said quickly, wanting to keep the distance between the two of them. "I hope you have not forgotten the agreement we made when we entered this marriage. I would not want you to be under the illusion that I intend to share my life with you."

She flinched as though he had struck her, and when pain flickered in her gray eyes, he pushed away the rifling in his gut. This was what they'd agreed to and, even though they'd been married now for over a month, he had no intention of changing his ways. All in all, he'd made very few changes to his life, and while Christina now resided with him, she lived her life, and he lived his.

Daniel did not want to allow any feelings to continue growing for his wife, which meant that the less he saw of her, the better. If she were not in his company, then he would not have to battle the unwanted, unwelcome feelings that had been rising of late.

He had always thought, since their first meeting, that Christina was not a particular beauty but, ever since the day she'd stepped into the church in her wedding finery, he'd struggled not to think of her subdued beauty during quiet moments — and he hated that weakness within him.

"I understand, Daniel," Christina said, slowly, her eyes searching his own as her anger seemed to fade away, replaced with a deep sadness that Daniel knew he was responsible for. "I just wondered if we ought to be seen by the *ton* since we have not been out together yet."

He shrugged. "I care very little for the *ton* and what they think," he replied, turning his head away from her so that he could pick up one of the many sheets of paper on his desk, letting his eyes fall on the words but not managing to read it while Christina was in the room with him, distracting him. "Besides, I am sure they will believe us to be enjoying one another's company, if you get my meaning."

He hated the heat that climbed up his spine and rushed into his neck and face as he spoke. He had intended to be matter of fact but now, it appeared, he was embarrassed to be mentioning such a thing to his wife. Slowly, he let his gaze slide from the paper up toward her, only to see that she had dropped her eyes to the carpet, her cheeks a dark pink. Perhaps this would be the end of the matter. Perhaps he had embarrassed her enough that she might take her leave of his company. He could only hope. Alas, Christina was a straightforward sort of woman.

"And when are you going to enjoy my company, Daniel?"

Her quiet words stunned him, the paper sliding from his fingers as he stared at her in shock.

"I have been waiting for you," she said, frankly. "It has been weeks and you have still not come to consummate our marriage."

Daniel felt his mouth go dry as he stared at his wife, seeing the steadiness in her gaze as she spoke. He certainly had never expected her to discuss this with him, and he wasn't quite sure what to make of it or how to respond.

"I want you to come to my bed, Daniel — or, if you wish, I will come to yours. You need only ask me."

"Why?"

His voice was hoarse, his palms growing sweaty as he pressed them together under the table. The thought of having Christina in his bed had, of course, occurred to him more than once. He had wanted to go to her, had found himself thinking of her, desiring her, but he had never acted on those thoughts. It would be wrong, he'd told himself, for he was beginning to feel affection for her, affection he didn't want to admit. To love her physically would not only draw her closer, but it could push Laura out of his heart entirely.

Recently his thoughts of her were slowly fading. A couple of days would go by and he'd be sitting by the fire, drinking brandy, only to realize that he couldn't remember her face anymore and that he'd not had a single thought about her in as many days.

Shame burned through him.

"We are husband and wife," Christina began, spreading her hands as though this ought to be a simple matter for him to understand. "It is something I expect and something I believe you confirmed to me would occur should we marry. How else are you to beget an heir?" She looked at him carefully, her eyes narrowing just a little. "Is there something wrong with me?"

"No, no," Daniel exclaimed, his gaze traveling down the length of his wife, taking in her gentle curves and finding himself wondering what she would feel like underneath his hands. "No, it is not you. It is just that I have not wanted to... importune you."

Even as he made his excuse, Daniel knew it was a poor one and, from the look in Christina's eyes, she knew it was a lie.

"Whatever your reason, Daniel, I would like to have this marriage consummated, so that there can be nothing to separate us. I would... I would like to bear a child." She gave him a small, shy, imploring smile, her cheeks still reddening as she spoke. "I thought that, perhaps if we spent a little more time together, got to know one another a bit better, you might be more willing to come to my bed."

The hope in her expression poured guilt onto him in

waves. He had neglected her in so many ways but even still, the thought of going to her, to make love to her, terrified him. He didn't want to feel anything for her, didn't want to forget Laura or to open himself up to the risk of losing someone he loved again. And yet, she was right in that it was his duty to consummate this marriage and to hopefully conceive an heir.

He hated the desire that began to pool in him as Christina looked at him with those gentle gray eyes of hers, a few tendrils of her fair hair wisping around her temples as she studied him.

"Y-yes, well," he stammered, clearing his throat. "I will certainly think about it."

It was clearly not the answer she'd been hoping for, and the light in her eyes faded.

"If you will excuse me," Daniel muttered, leaning forward over his papers and knowing full well that he was pushing her away. "I am sure we can talk another time about these matters."

"Very well, Daniel," she murmured, turning away from him and making her way toward the door. "As you wish it."

"Enjoy your stroll."

She paused. "I will, thank you. And, Daniel…"

There was a pronounced silence and, despite his determination not to do so, Daniel looked up at his bride. She was standing at the door, one hand on the handle and the other loose by her side. The pain was still in her eyes, but also a glint of determination. There was no smile on her lips as she looked at him steadily.

"You are my husband, Daniel. I will be 'Christina' to you, not 'Lady Ravenhall.' It is much too formal. You are trying to keep me at arm's length, I know, but there is no need for such formality."

It was not a question but a statement, and Daniel found

himself staring after his wife as the door closed behind her. She knew what he was doing, knew full well that he did not want her company nor her support in his endeavors, and yet she was bearing it with good grace, and quite fairly pushing him for more.

Guilt rippled through him once more. He ought to have said yes, ought to have stepped away from his desk to take a walk with his wife, even if it were only for half an hour. She was right that they should show the *ton* that they were wonderfully happy in their hasty marriage, but Daniel found that he wanted to go with her simply to bring a smile to her face.

"And that is precisely the reason that I will stay where I am," he said aloud, one hand curling into a fist as he slammed it down, hard, onto the table. "Enough of this nonsense, Daniel. Leave your wife to live her own life, and you concentrate on your own."

Frowning, Daniel leaned over his desk and tried to review his documents, only to discover that his eyes would not focus. He could not so much as read a single word, tortured as he was by conflicting thoughts and feelings over his wife.

Groaning aloud, Daniel set his head down on the desk and squeezed his eyes closed. A familiar vision came to his mind, the vision of Laura walking just ahead of him, laughing softly as she strolled along a path surrounded by bright yellow daffodils.

Except, when she turned to face him, it was no longer Laura's face that he saw. It was Christina's.

CHAPTER 14

When Daniel thought of all the places in the world he could be at this very moment, a picnic in Hyde Park with his wife, his sister and her husband, and what seemed to be half the *ton* looking on was near the bottom of his list.

Had Polly addressed her note to *him* asking them to attend, he would have refused before he had even reached the end of it. But no, his sister was much smarter than that, and instead had sent it to Christina, who very gladly accepted on their behalf. He had told her in no uncertain terms that he would not be attending, but when she told him she would ask Lord Hudson to escort her, and wouldn't that give the *ton* something to talk about, he finally resigned himself to the fact that he would be spending a day outdoors with some of the worst people in all of London.

Though he had to admit, his wife certainly seemed happy. Christina, Polly, and Lady Beatrice were chatting away animatedly in front of him, while Daniel brooded as Hudson and his brother-in-law, Lord Taylor, spoke around him.

"Ravenhall, it is jolly good to see you out and about," said

Taylor. "We are family, it's true, and yet I feel as though I hardly know you. Why, Polly says—"

Daniel shot him a withering glare that quelled any further conversation. He had little interest in what Polly had to say. He knew his sister, the youngest and therefore the one who didn't even remember Daniel as a child, found him somewhat fascinating, a fact which disconcerted him.

Taylor forged on. "Yes. Well, that is to say—"

"If you will excuse me, gentlemen, I must speak with my wife."

Daniel increased his speed, quickly reaching the women, and he leaned down to speak into Christina's ear.

"Lady Ravenhall, would you allow me to escort you the rest of the way?" he asked, gesturing down the path they were to travel to reach the picnic destination.

Her eyes widened, and he realized she had never known the Daniel who could flirt, who enjoyed the small, trivial things that seemed to matter to his peers.

"Of course," she responded, her hand coming to his arm as they broke away slightly from the other women.

"Thank you for agreeing to come," she said, though he knew she was fully aware he had no intentions of attending until she had forced his hand. "I do appreciate the opportunity to become better acquainted with your family and to spend more time at events."

"Yes. Well," he shrugged. "This will not be a typical occurrence, you do understand? At some point, I will be returning to the country. Though if you would like to stay in London, I suppose it could be arranged."

She turned her serene stare upon him and shook her head. "No, Daniel, I think it is better that we reside together."

"Very well," he said with a shrug, though why she was adamant about this, he wasn't sure. "Once this threat is gone, then we will return to the country. You'll like my estate, I think. It's fairly peaceful, and the villagers are welcoming. Hopefully, you shouldn't be bored."

"No," she said with a shake of her head. "I enjoy taking care of a household and living in the country. I look forward to it."

"Good," he said, before lapsing into silence, unsure of what else to say to her.

"Daniel," she began, and he nearly groaned aloud. This was why he kept his distance. While she was practical, she also liked to put everything out into the open between them, while he preferred to tamp down whatever he was feeling. But, fortunately, she kept emotions out of this particular conversation. "Tell me more of your... work. I mean, I know that you have these houses for women and children, but what else do you do?"

He sighed, wondering how much to tell her, but, seeing she was truly interested, he began.

"You know the circumstances that began my interest in seeing others find justice," he said, his face grim. "It began when I was... at a low point, and leaving a club in St. Giles one night. It was shortly after Laura's death, and I didn't know what to do, where to go. So for a time I did what most men did, drowned myself in drink. Although I was on the hunt for Northcliffe, he seemingly had disappeared. Anyway, I walked out into the street and there was a young woman carrying a child, running as though her life depended on getting away. Which it did."

He cleared his throat, feeling the intensity of Christina's captivated stare.

"Her husband was chasing her, and he had nearly caught her, but I stumbled into his path accidentally. He ran into me and we both fell in the mud. He was momentarily stunned, and I picked up the woman and lifted her and the child into my waiting carriage so they could escape him. But when I asked her where to go, she gave her home address — right back to where the bastard lived. He drank too much, he was abusive, but if she left him, she would starve. So I allowed her to come back to my townhouse. Gave them both something to eat and told her she couldn't go back, couldn't allow her child to be raised in such a house. But then I faced the dilemma of what to do with her. And so—" He raised his hands in front of him. "That's how it began. Typically, it's women and children. Sometimes orphans, sometimes entire families who need shelter, or anyone who needs someone to help them out of their current situations. And then I keep them from ever being hurt by the same person again if required. If they have been wronged, I make things right."

She turned sharply to look at him but didn't ask any questions, apparently not wanting to know any more, which he was happy about. Somehow, telling her and her good soul about his darkness in the brilliant light of the day seemed wrong.

Christina was quiet for a moment, and he wondered what she was thinking of him and his work. Would she judge him for it? Did she think him too high a peer for doing what he did? Could she—?

"I think what you do for those people is admirable," she said, looking at him with wonder. "Not many people would give their time or their wealth to such a cause."

"Hudson does most of the work," he said with a shrug, not wanting her praise. He helped others, sure, but he did it to help himself feel better.

"Even still," she said with a smile and patted his hand. "You're a good person, Daniel."

"I wish you wouldn't say that to me," he said, grimacing, hoping to keep her from furthering the subject.

"Truly," she said. "I know there is some darkness inside you, but nothing that can't be recovered from."

He sighed as he looked around, glad when he realized they'd reached the picnic site. His sister came bounding up behind them, her smile alighting on Christina.

"We have the perfect place for ourselves," she said with a grin and led them over to where her maid was laying out a blanket. Polly sat next to her husband, and Daniel led Christina over to occupy space next to Lady Beatrice.

"No," she whispered to him. "Allow Lord Hudson to sit next to her."

He was taken aback by her comment, but he looked up to see Hudson sending a wink his way, and suddenly he was aware of the way the two of them stared at one another. Well, well, it seemed Hudson was smitten with the Lady Beatrice. She was a stunning woman, to be sure, tiny, with dark, good looks, but Daniel found no attraction to her whatsoever. No, it seemed he now preferred women with sandy blonde hair that glowed in the sun, who had curves that fit beautifully into his hands. He wanted Christina. The thought punched him in the gut, and when he looked down at her, he felt a stirring within him.

No, Daniel, he warned himself, pushing the lust back, and sat down next to her for the lunch.

Alas, it was torture. She was so near him, and she kept leaning over his lap for various dainties and sandwiches. A couple of times, he nearly groaned aloud. When Hudson gave him a knowing look, he frowned at him, causing his friend to laugh.

"What is it?" Lady Beatrice asked, to which Hudson shook his head.

"Nothing at all," he said. "Just having a bit of fun at my friend, here."

"At Daniel?" Polly said, wide-eyed. "Daniel never has fun."

"Hush, love," said Taylor, to Daniel's great relief.

Taking note that they had finished their food, Daniel

stood and announced he was going for a walk to further explore these particular gardens.

"I'll accompany you," Christina said, beginning to rise, but Daniel held up a hand.

"I'm fine alone," he said, but when he felt five pairs of accusing eyes trained on him, he nodded in agreement.

"It is lovely here, isn't it?" Christina asked as they began.

He nodded again, rather stupidly. Her close proximately wasn't helping matters, as he was trying to thrust her and her luscious body from his thoughts.

"I suppose," he finally answered, as they pushed deeper into the trees, away from the eyes of society. He didn't want to be under scrutiny as he spoke to his wife. But now that they were well away, completely alone under the canopy of trees, he realized he had no desire to talk. No, he wanted to do far more than that.

Turning so suddenly that Christina let out a gasp, he pulled her to him, his hands cradling her face and tilting her chin up toward him. His lips met hers hurriedly, and she gave a slight moan of pleasure that sent heat streaking through him.

"Christina," he murmured, his hands roaming over her, seeking out satiny, velvety skin that seemed to be calling to him. Her hands came to his elbows, pulling him closer, her lips and tongue, while inexperienced, drawing him in further to her depths. He felt her ample chest against him, and he wanted to release her breasts and see how they would look in the sunlight.

This pleasure could be had all the time, a little voice told him, but he tried to shut that voice away and concentrate on the moment itself. He deepened the kiss, suddenly taking control as he swept his tongue over hers. So many nights the thought of Christina in her bed just down the hallway tortured him, and now that the door had opened, all of the pent-up passion he had restrained came pouring out into the kiss. He had known he wanted Christina, he just didn't realize how badly he did.

Suddenly nearby laughter broke through his consciousness, and the realization of where they were came rushing back. Good Lord, he'd just about taken his wife here in the middle of Hyde Park.

"Christina, I am so sorry," he said, raking a hand through his hair.

"There are many things to be sorry for," she said quietly. "But that is not one of them. Come to my bed, Daniel," she whispered, and before he could say anything in response, she was gone.

CHAPTER 15

*C*hristina sighed as she walked, glad that the London streets were still fairly quiet. She had always been accustomed to walking out alone, enjoying the fresh air and the time to herself, but there was something about being married and alone that felt very different. She could not explain it, not even to herself, yet it lingered there in her heart.

It had been another two weeks since she and Daniel had shared any lovely moments together, following their day at the picnic. She could hardly believe she had brought up the subject of consummating their marriage, but something had to be done. Even though her cheeks still burned at the thought of what she'd said, Christina did not regret being so honest with her husband. The difficulty was, despite their passionate kiss in the park, now over a fortnight on, he still had not appeared in her bedchamber. She no longer saw him often at dinner anymore either and, even on the nights they did eat together, he was quiet and distant.

As Christina continued to find herself longing for more, she cursed her foolish heart. After all, she had agreed to this marriage, knowing what he felt — or didn't feel — for her, but she had never considered that she would find it so difficult. She had believed that life would be just the same as it was prior to this, when she had been at home with her father, but she was beginning to realize how much had changed.

Christina walked through the door of the bookshop, inhaling the comforting, woody scent of leather-bound books. The interior was dim, and the light that shone in from high windows shimmered off the dust in the air. She smiled at the bookshop owner as she began to wander.

When she had been at her former home, there had never been the desire to spend time in her father's company, for she had found him brash, somewhat heartless, and inclined to talk about himself.

Her husband was practically silent, as though he had no interest in sharing anything about himself with her, but she found herself craving his company regardless. It did not help that she was often caught with the memory of his kisses — first in the gardens all those weeks ago and then the sudden kiss at the picnic. She found her hand drifting to her lips as she recalled just how wonderfully shocking it had been. As much as she wanted him in her bed to have children, her heart also quickened as she thought of his lips upon hers once more.

Of course, being untouched, she had no experience of what actually occurred between a husband and wife. Christina's mother had died when she was but a young child and she had no woman in her life to ask.

Instead, Beatrice had, in hushed tones, hastily described the act to her before Christina had married Daniel. Apparently, Beatrice had been told as much by her older sister in preparation for her own wedding, whenever that should come about. To Christina, it all sounded rather painful and hugely embarrassing to be as naked as the day you were born with another person, but Beatrice had informed her, in no uncertain terms, that her husband would require her to be unclad. That had sent shivers down her spine, her mind suddenly filled with questions as to what Daniel might expect and what he would think of her.

Sighing to herself, Christina wandered along the row of books, her fingers idly making their way along the spines as she walked. She enjoyed visiting this wonderful shop, filled with rows upon rows of more volumes than one could ever ask for, but she could find nothing to interest her today.

"Can I be of assistance to you, my lady?"

Christina jumped as the voice startled her, and looked up to see a gentleman leaning against the bookshelf in front of her wearing a warm smile on his face. He was not *un*handsome, although his smile did not reach his eyes. He was impeccably dressed, his mousey brown hair neatly styled, and his dark eyes pinning her where she stood.

"I am quite at my leisure this afternoon, sir," Christina replied, calmly, finding it very strange that a gentleman should speak to her without a proper introduction. "Do excuse me."

"That was rude of me, I apologize," the gentleman replied, stepping into Christina's way as she made to move farther into the bookshop. "I was simply caught by your beauty, my lady."

"Lady Ravenhall," she replied, firmly, turning her head to look at him directly, refusing to be intimidated by his gaze. "But as we have not yet been introduced, I do not think it wise to continue our conversation."

"Quite right," he grinned, leaning heavily on his cane. "Lady Ravenhall, you say. You must be the young woman who recently wed my old friend, Daniel?"

Seeing that she could not easily get past him, Christina sighed inwardly and made to turn around, only for the gentleman to capture her wrist. Her breath caught as she turned back to him, wrenching her arm away as perspiration broke out on her brow and she resisted the urge to flee from the man as fast as she could.

"Do excuse me, sir," she said, in a voice that she hoped did not shake. "And may I suggest that you do not touch me again. I am not obliged to speak with you." She jumped as she heard the door scrape open, allowing another person to enter the shop. Christina's initial relief fled when she realized they were too far hidden in the recesses of the bookshop to be seen from the entrance.

"Forgive me. It is just that I have been very eager to make your acquaintance," the gentleman replied, leaning forward so that Christina was forced to press herself back against the bookshelves. "After all, I have known your husband for a long time."

It was not his words that had Christina's heart clutching with an icy fear, but rather the look in the man's eyes. His smile had turned cruel, his narrowed eyes heartless and the tone of his voice mocking.

"You — you are Lord Northcliffe," she whispered.

The man chuckled. "So he married someone who has a decent head on her shoulders! Very observant, Lady Ravenhall. You need not fear anything from me, my lady, so you do not look so afraid. I am simply showing you and your husband that I have no intention of going anywhere and that his threats do not frighten me. I was called away on business for a short time, but I have returned to London and intend to do all I can to enjoy the remainder of the Season — hopefully without Lord Ravenhall's presence."

He reached up and brushed Christina's cheek gently, making her shudder. "You will tell him that you saw me, won't you, Lady Ravenhall?"

"Christina!"

The sound of Beatrice's voice shattered the tension between Christina and Lord Northcliffe and, as Christina turned to face her friend, she sensed Lord Northcliffe's presence vanish from beside her.

"There you are! When I called upon you, your butler said you could be found here. What a delightful shop this is. I must confess I do not visit it nearly often enough. And that dress is altogether lovely!" Beatrice exclaimed, a smile wreathed on her face as she came toward Christina. Her smile wavered as she drew closer, however, apparently seeing Christina's expression. "Are you all right? Who was it you were talking to? Is your husband here with you?"

Christina clutched Beatrice's arm, feeling a bit weak at the knees as she drew in deep breaths in an attempt to calm herself.

"Good heavens, whatever is the matter, Christina?" Beatrice asked again, sounding puzzled as the smile faded from her face. "Have you had some kind of shock?"

Christina swallowed hard, closing her eyes and attempting to rein in her emotions. "I was accosted by that gentleman," she said, becoming angry now as her fear passed, and she opened her eyes to look at Beatrice. "And no, Lord Ravenhall is not here. I did have a maid with me, but the poor thing looked ill as we began walking so I sent her home."

Lady Beatrice's eyes widened. "You were *accosted*? By whom?"

Christina opened her mouth to speak, only to close it again. Her husband had kept the information about Lord Northcliffe and Miss Churston to himself, with the exception of Lord Hudson, and it would not be right of her to speak to Lady Beatrice about it.

"I — I am not sure," she said, as the door to the bookshop opened again. "Someone who, I think, believed I might be free with my favors now that I am a married woman."

Beatrice gasped, her cheeks burning rosy red. "That is truly awful!" she exclaimed, grasping Christina's hand. "You must return home at once. Did you bring a carriage?"

Christina shook her head. "I walked."

"Come with me and we shall return you home," Beatrice replied, gesturing to her maid to follow her as they left the bookshop. "It has been an age since we last spoke, Christina, and I so wanted to catch up with you, which is why I was seeking you out."

"I have missed you as well, Beatrice," Christina replied as they walked out to the street. "You must come for afternoon tea tomorrow. I insist upon it. It has been too long since we have talked."

Beatrice smiled, seeming genuinely pleased with the thought. "That would be wonderful."

Feeling a good deal better now that she was out in the fresh air, Christina drew in a deep breath and settled her shoulders. "What has been keeping you occupied as of late? Have you any gentlemen to speak of yourself, Beatrice? I am sure there are many who are keen to court you."

Beatrice shook her head as they approached her carriage. "No, not yet. I believe my personality is a little too loud for many of the gentlemen who are looking for a bride. Mama is always telling me that I must calm myself down but as much as I try, there is very little I can do!"

Christina smiled softly. "You will find someone very soon, I am sure," she replied, glad that the memory of Lord Northcliffe was being chased away by Lady Beatrice's conversation. "And you need not change who you are to find him either."

Just as she was about to climb into Beatrice's carriage, she was interrupted by the sound of her name being called.

Turning her head, she saw Lord Hudson waving at her from his curricle.

"Lady Ravenhall!" he exclaimed as he brought his horses to a halt and stepped down from his seat. "How good to see you! I was just on my way to your home, to speak with that husband of yours."

"Lovely to see you as well, Lord Hudson," she said. "Lady Beatrice was going to see me home, but if you are going that way, I will not trouble her, if you do not mind."

"Of course not," he said with a warm smile and a prolonged glance at Beatrice, which Christina noted with amusement. "I would appreciate the company."

"Lady Beatrice, you remember Lord Hudson?" Christina asked.

"Absolutely," Beatrice replied, her eyes brightening as she smiled at Lord Hudson. "From the wedding and then at the picnic."

He beamed at Beatrice. "It would be difficult to forget you, my lady. You were a wonderful dancer, if I recall correctly, and an excellent lunch companion." As he helped Christina into the curricle, Christina was interested to notice that his eyes never left her friend.

"I do hope I will have the opportunity to dance with you again, Lady Beatrice," Lord Hudson continued, seeming reluctant to leave her to join Christina in the carriage. "Or perhaps you might enjoy a short walk in the park one afternoon?"

Christina smiled to herself as she watched from atop the curricle. Beatrice colored furiously but nodded, her expression a little shy. Apparently, Lord Hudson was interested in furthering his acquaintance with Beatrice and, privately, Christina thought they would make a good match, as they were both as cheerfully loud as the other.

"A lovely lady, your friend," Lord Hudson commented as

he stepped and sat down, taking the reins in hand while Christina waved goodbye to Beatrice. "I always meant to call on her but I had not yet had the opportunity what with all I have been engaged in recently."

Christina lifted one eyebrow. "Helping those who cannot help themselves?"

Lord Hudson grinned. "Precisely. I'm sure Ravenhall has told you all about it but we have been able to secure a third establishment to rent for those who require a place to stay away from drunken husbands and the like. All quite secure, and the sewing and washing will be brought in as a means of payment for the women who are able. That husband of yours is quite something, Christina."

Nodding, Christina looked out at the passing houses, thinking how strange it was that Lord Hudson appeared to know more than she did regarding her husband's actions over the past few weeks.

"Yes," she murmured, her eyes glazing over with a sudden sheen of tears. "Yes, he really is something, Lord Hudson."

CHAPTER 16

*D*aniel yawned widely as he leaned back in his office chair and stretched, thinking that it was likely time for him to retire. He had already tossed his jacket and cravat on the chair across the desk, though he knew his valet would most likely have a fit over the state of his clothing come the morning.

Daniel had been surprised when Christina had returned from her walk with Lord Hudson earlier that afternoon, but of course, he welcomed his friend and, once their conversation was over, Daniel had insisted that Hudson remain for dinner.

He had regretted it, however, when he saw the way Christina laughed with Hudson, smiling at him and responding to his witty conversation. He knew there was nothing between the two of them, and yet, he couldn't help the envy that crept over him, as he wished that *he* was the recipient of her sparkling eyes and meaningful conversation.

It was better that she remained at a distance, he reminded himself. He couldn't help but notice, however, that in moments of silence she seemed somewhat restless, pushing food around her plate and fiddling with the simple gold band around her finger. Following dinner, she retired early, leaving him and Hudson with their port.

Guilt crept through his veins as Daniel realized he had been caught up with his own feelings of jealousy and entertaining his guest when he should have likely ensured that his wife was not unwell. He had bade her goodnight and left things there, not once thinking to go and check on her, nor considering speaking with her to find out if something was the matter.

Mayhap she just has a headache, he told himself, throwing back the rest of his port. *And she will be asleep by now, anyway. There is no need to trouble her.*

Rising from his chair, Daniel wandered to the window and looked down at the streets of Mayfair below, though his mind was now filled with thoughts of his wife. He had been doing so well these last few weeks, ensuring he spent as much time away from her as possible, forcing her from his mind without too much difficulty, but it was taking more and more effort to do so since he was often caught up in thinking of her. He did not want her in this thoughts, did not want his heart to quicken whenever she came into a room, did not want desire to pool in his core when she smiled at him — and yet it seemed he could no more keep his emotions under control than he could keep from breathing. Needing to speak of it, he had finally expressed some of his thoughts to Hudson earlier that evening, but the man had simply laughed at him, clearly not fully understanding his distress.

"Laura is no longer with you, Ravenhall," Hudson finally said with more compassion, when he realized that Daniel was actually serious, and Daniel wished he had never said anything, as he didn't want to be pitied. "You have done right by her, but it is time to move on, to find happiness for yourself. You have every right to fall in love with your wife, you know. In fact, I would heartily recommend it."

Frustrated, though at who and for what he wasn't sure, Daniel threw his head back and stared at the ceiling, his eyes closing tightly. This was not what he'd intended. He'd thought to remain aloof and entirely unaffected by his wife, believing that he'd be able to consummate his marriage without any kind of emotion bubbling up through him, but now he knew it would be impossible. Perhaps that was why he'd stepped back from going to her bed, why he'd stopped himself from doing the one thing he ought.

No one will ever again have my heart, he vowed trying to convince himself as he opened his eyes and looked back out onto the road. *What you feel for Christina is desire. Nothing more.*

"Daniel?"

Jerking in surprise, Daniel turned to see Christina standing framed in the doorway. She was in her nightdress, with no kind of dressing gown wrapped around her to hide her form from him. As she walked toward him, Daniel came to his feet, his breath hitching in his throat as he saw the outline of her curves through the thin material, the swift kick of desire catching him unaware.

"What are you doing here, Christina?" he ground out as she reached him, but cut his words off when she looked up at him.

Her eyes were red-rimmed and filled with unshed tears, her lip trembling just a little.

Concern filled him. Why had she been crying? He didn't think but reached out his hand toward her, and she caught it with her own, clenching it as if drawing strength from him. To his surprise, she leaned into him and rested her head on his shoulder, even though he had not invited the contact. For a moment, he stood still, unsure of what to do as he felt her body soft and warm against him. He meant to put his hands against her to gently push her back away from him, but it seemed his arms acted of their own accord, as they slowly wrapped around her shoulders, his hands rubbing her back as she sighed, sniffling just a little.

"What's the matter, Christina?" he asked, gently, pushing away the sudden, ferocious desire to look down into her eyes, take her lips, and kiss away whatever was troubling her with all of the passion and desire that had been building within him for weeks now. "Is this why you left the table earlier this evening?"

She nodded, her head rubbing against his shirt. "I saw Lord Northcliffe today," she said, and his blood turned to ice in his veins as he froze in place, his heart seeming to come to a stop for a moment.

"He knew who I was and where to find me," Christina continued softly. "He — he frightened me."

Daniel swallowed hard, fear and anger fighting to take control of him, but he knew it was more important to be there for Christina.

"He said to tell you that he had been called away from London for a time on business, but that he has returned again with no intention of leaving, despite your threats." Christina lifted her head and looked up at him, and Daniel saw how she tried valiantly to keep her chin from quivering as her eyes searched his for reassurance. "How did he know who I was?"

Drawing in a long breath, Daniel let it out slowly as he tried to stay as calm as he could. "He will have made it his business to find out. Lord Northcliffe and I... we have been something of competitors since our school days as boys. We were consistently besting one another. When I fell for Laura, I didn't know that he had already developed affections for her. Apparently, that was just more than he could take.

Anyway, I'm not sure what further I can do to keep him away until I can prove to the rest of society what he has done."

"I — I was afraid of him," Christina admitted, biting her lip. "I didn't know what to do, but luckily Lady Beatrice arrived and Lord Northcliffe seemed to vanish."

"Why did you not speak of this before now?" he asked, confused now. "Lord Hudson knows Lord Northcliffe, and he would have understood your need to tell me everything."

She shook her head, her eyes drifting closed. "I did not want him to see me upset," she replied, her head now leaning on his shoulder again, her breath whispering across his neck. "I wanted only to speak to you."

There was such vulnerability in her words, in her openness, that Daniel could not help but respond, and warmth spread through his body in the knowledge that he was the one she trusted. His arms tightened around her in a sudden, fierce possessiveness, his eyes closing as he battled the emotions running wild through him. There rose in him such a ruthless protectiveness that he felt as though it might take charge of him completely, in his anger that Northcliffe had chosen to frighten Christina as a way to get at Daniel.

"This is not your fault," Christina whispered, her hands reaching up to slide around his neck, her fingers threading through his hair. "Do not blame yourself, Daniel."

He couldn't speak for a moment, his blood pounding wildly as he fought the furious desire rushing through him, the desire that swept all other emotions away. He wanted to remain angry with Lord Northcliffe, wanted to stay enraged with him for what he had done, but all he could think was just how much he wanted his wife.

She stilled in his arms as he lowered his head, brushing her temple with his lips while inwardly cursing himself. He knew he had to bed her, but this was not how he'd intended to do it. There had been the thought that he'd remain entirely aloof, as though he could separate his heart from his body as he lay with her, but he couldn't ignore the deep, unquenchable emotion that filled him. He was fond of his wife, he realized, otherwise he would not be so upset by what she had told him. He was angry that Lord Northcliffe had frightened Christina, that he'd used her as a pawn in whatever cruel game he was playing — but the urge to protect Christina, to reassure her and take away her fear, grew with every second that he held her in his arms and became more important than any vengeance.

He stepped away, suddenly desperate to break their connection. He couldn't do this. Not now, not when he had lost all control over his emotions.

Christina looked up at him, her face filled with confusion, her arms falling to her sides. She swallowed hard, her lips trembling as a sheen came over her eyes, more tears threatening to fall from them.

"Daniel," she whispered, stepping toward him. "Don't turn away from me."

Daniel wanted to say no, wanted to leave her, but it was as if an invisible cord pulled him toward his wife, to her lush beauty, her caring heart, her practical, rational mind. Closing his eyes, he fought hard, but it was of no use. He had to surrender to what he felt.

Without thinking about what he was doing, he stepped toward her suddenly and slammed his mouth down over hers. The passion that swiftly took over surprised him and Christina responded to him in kind, her body shivering as he held her tightly.

If you give into this desire, then nothing will ever be the same again.

He ignored the voice inside his head, forgot the memory of his first love and his fear of loving again, and chose to let his passion overrule it all. The feeling of her lips on his burned hot fire through his body, and Daniel knew he was lost.

His hands began to roam up her back, his lips leaving her mouth to touch the curve of her throat. She gasped, and one of her hands tightened around his neck. He didn't stop, couldn't stop, but instead lifted her bodily into his arms and strode from the room and up the stairs.

CHAPTER 17

*H*er bedchamber was warm, with only a few candles and a fire burning in the hearth. Daniel did not put Christina down until he reached her bed, easing her back gently as he kissed her again.

There was no need to ask her if she wanted this, not when he heard her quiet moan as he ran his hand down the length of her body. Reminding himself that she was innocent, Daniel lifted himself up from her for a moment, looking down into her eyes as they fluttered open.

"Do not leave me, Daniel," she whispered, her eyes bright in the candlelight. "Please, don't leave me. Not now. I need you."

His heart cried out that he needed her just as much, but he did not say a word to her. Instead, he pushed his hands into her hair, marveling at how easily it came free of the long braid she'd tied it in. It was lit by the flames in the grate, shimmering with gold and bronze, and he savored the feel of the silken strands running through his fingers as he spread her hair out across the bed.

Goodness, she was glorious.

His fingers found the buttons of her nightgown and, without hesitating, he began to pluck them open. Christina inhaled sharply as his hands touched the bare flesh beneath. Desire burned through him as he let his mouth trail down her neck, her collarbone and, finally, to her breasts.

Christina nearly came off the bed as he touched her, her mouth opening but no sound emerging. Never before had he wanted a woman so badly, and he was suddenly desperate to see her in all of her naked glory.

"Take it off," he growled, sitting up to unbutton his shirt. She looked at him with wide eyes, her hair tumbling around her shoulders as she sat up.

"Don't hide from me," he muttered as she lifted her hands to cover her breasts. He knew he should be softer with her, whisper tender words that would make her feel comfortable, but he was so overcome that it didn't seem as if he could say anything to convey how he felt. "You are my wife. I want to see you."

He did not ask again but continued to divest himself of his clothing, aware of her quiet gasp as he flung the last of his undergarments to the floor.

Remember, she is untouched.

The reminder had him stilling, looking over at his now naked wife, seeing the trepidation mixed with desire in her eyes.

"You do not need to be afraid," he said slowly, trying to be patient in order to calm her fears as he climbed back onto the bed and settled himself beside her instead of atop. "I'm aware this is new for you, but I'll make it good for you — I promise."

She swallowed, turning her head to look into his eyes as he let his hand trail across her breasts, and his body roared to life once more. He could not look away as he let his hand reach farther down her soft skin, wanting to see the expression on her face as he touched her very core.

She jerked, her face burning with color and her eyes widening as he pressed his finger against her soft folds.

"Daniel! I — I'm not sure—"

"There is nothing shameful in what you feel," he said softly, trying his best to rein in his burning passion before he took her without any consideration for her own enjoyment. "You are so beautiful, Christina."

He was shocked when tears fell from her eyes as they closed, and he lifted his hand from her, his passion ebbing away as he heard her sob.

"Christina," he breathed, not quite sure what to say. "I'm sorry. I didn't mean...."

She shook her head, opening her eyes and grasping his hand, bringing it to her mouth before pressing a gentle kiss to his knuckles. "I'm sorry, Daniel. It's just that—" She broke off and sat up, looking away from him for a moment as she seemed to attempt to regain her composure. "It is just that no one has ever said that to me before. My father has always told me that I am barely tolerable, so to hear those words from your lips — whether you mean them or not — well, it means more than you know."

A surge of anger burst through Daniel's heart as he took in Christina's soft, sad smile, and he thought how unjust it was that no one had appreciated her beauty before.

"Of course I mean it," he replied, gently reaching to brush away her tears and marveling at how soft she was beneath his touch. "Just look at you, Christina. You are glorious."

She smiled at him then, her tears diminishing, and she was the only woman present in Daniel's thoughts as he considered that he had never seen someone so lovely before.

As they looked into one another's eyes, Daniel felt his heart break open, the pain and grief of the past beginning to wash away as the affection he saw in Christina's gaze swept a sense of healing into him.

Christina kissed him then, taking him by surprise. Leaning forward, she let herself settle against him, and, with a tug, Daniel pulled her on top of himself. She did not gasp, did not cry out, but continued to let her lips rove over him, becoming the aggressor as she leaned down so that her breasts were pressed against his chest.

He drank her in, his hands running over her gentle curves as his hardness now pressed against her soft entrance. He found himself aching for her, and he forced himself to remain still while she explored his body, though her actions only tantalized him all the more.

Her hips moved and Daniel groaned, aware of Christina's surprise — although whether that was from his ferocity or her own mounting pleasure, he could not say. His blood surged as she sat up, looking down at him as her fingers skimmed lightly over his chest.

Her skin seemed to glow in the firelight, her hair falling down about her shoulders and breasts. She was a goddess. Daniel reached out one hand and carefully pressed it between where their bodies met, hearing her explosive intake of breath as he touched her again.

"Give in to it," he murmured, as she began to rock of her own accord. "Don't hold yourself back."

It took all of his strength not to lift her up and make her his, but Daniel forced himself to wait until she reached her crescendo. Her eyes were closed, her head thrown back and, as he continued his ministrations, her body tensed.

A loud moan emanated from her throat, and her breathing became as ragged as his. With his other hand, he reached up to caress one of her breasts. Even lost in the sensations, he heard her cry out in release. Wrapping his arms around her, he rested her back on the bed and, without hesitating, pushed himself inside.

She cried out, biting her lip, and Daniel remained still for a moment, as much as it tortured him.

"It will pass in a moment," he said softly, aware that her pain would be sharp but that it shouldn't linger.

"You are mine now, Christina," he said more fiercely now, overcome by the euphoria that rushed over him at the thought.

Her eyes fluttered open, and she looked into his face, her pained expression slowly fading.

"You are so beautiful," he whispered again, knowing what the words meant to her as he ran one finger lightly down her cheek and began to move slowly, waves of bliss rippling through him with each thrust. He had not allowed himself this release for years and found moans escaping from his mouth just as they had done from Christina's.

The pleasure built with an intensity he had never before experienced, his body tightening as he struggled to keep control of himself. Stars exploded in his mind as he gripped the sheets on either side of her head, and he opened his eyes to drink her in before, finally, his body bucked and writhed, and he emptied himself into her.

He had done it. Their marriage was consummated at last — and yet, deep within him, Daniel felt a desire for Christina begin to build in him again. It was as though his passions could not be sated by one single encounter, as though he would need her again and again.

Slowly drawing back, he lay down next to his wife, knowing she was studying him but finding himself unable to return her gaze, afraid of what he would see in her eyes. Staring up at the top of her four-poster bed, Christina curled up next to him, her head resting on his shoulder and one arm thrown across his chest.

"I love you, Daniel," she told him softly.

He froze, staring unblinkingly at one of the bedposts. Had he truly just heard those words from her? Or had they been in his own imagination?

Had they been the memory of Laura whispering those very same words into his ear?

Closing his eyes, Daniel's body cooled, his shame beginning to mount an assault upon him once more. He had taken Christina to bed, but he had let his emotions roam free as he had done so. He had allowed himself to *feel*, to grow warm with affection for the lady who now lay drifting to sleep beside him.

He had betrayed all the promises he had made to himself, and he groaned in realization of the folly of his actions. This was why he had kept his distance, what he was afraid could happen.

Out of nowhere, Hudson's words echoed through his mind. *She is no longer with you, Daniel. You have every right to fall in love with your wife.*

He closed his eyes tightly, reaching to pull the sheet up around Christina. He did not want to feel anything for her, not when he had vowed never to love another. And it wasn't fair for her to love him, either, for it would only set her up for heartbreak. This was wrong. He was bringing shame to Laura's memory, was forgetting his promises.

Slipping out of bed, he looked down at Christina, seeing her blonde tresses spread out across the pillow behind her. He'd meant it when he'd told her she was beautiful, and anger still niggled him over what her father had told her. Even now, after falling into an exhausted sleep, she was lovely. Daniel could not remember ever seeing something so exquisite.

And yet, he had to turn away from her. Until he had found justice for Laura's death, he could never allow himself to forget his first love, nor the vows he had made. Christina would just have to understand that. She could never mean anything to him.

All he had to do was force himself to believe it.

CHAPTER 18

When she awoke only a few hours later, Christina had been disheartened to discover that Daniel was no longer in her bed. The place where he'd lain was cold, meaning he'd left her chamber some time ago.

Her heart had grown heavy, and tears began to leak down her cheeks until she finally fell into a fitful sleep for a few hours, only to wake with a pounding head and an aching chest.

Now, dressed and eating breakfast, she reflected on all that had taken place last evening. She had never meant to seduce Daniel, but she had sought him out to tell him of her encounter with Lord Northcliffe, and, she realized, to seek comfort.

When they had finally consummated their marriage, she thought that she had broken through the wall he'd built around himself, that she had found a place in his heart, regardless of the past. She had thought that the man from last evening was the man she'd known dwelt underneath all that silence. He had been warm and tender, passionate and gentle as he'd led her through her first experience of love-making. Her emotions had roared to life as he'd touched her, and she had been shocked to find herself in the throes of passion as she opened herself up to reveal all she felt.

And now, this morning, she felt alive yet broken. As she sat here alone, she wondered if it had all been nothing more than imaginings created inside her head. Daniel had found physical satisfaction with her, to be sure, but meanwhile, she had completely and utterly lost her heart.

How, she didn't know. He was rude, callous, standoffish, and yet there were times when she saw a completely different side of him. She saw the man who cared more for helping those in need than inheriting a dukedom. Sometimes, when Daniel didn't know she was looking, a haunted look passed over his face, as though he was struggling to keep from giving in to the darkness that threatened. And still, he took on the role of protector of others, put his family above all — why, he had married her in order to keep his family name intact as well as to continue his work. Somehow, she had found her way through a tiny gap in the wall he had built around his heart.

But could she truly live with such a man, who would cast away her love and just use her for her physical pleasure?

"Lady Christina! Good morning!"

Christina paused, her hand halfway to her mouth as she held the teacup in her hand. "Lord Hudson," she murmured, surprised to see him here so early. "What has brought you here this morning?"

"Your husband," Lord Hudson chuckled, as Daniel walked into the room, coming toward her. "He says he has something for us all to discuss."

Christina caught her breath as Daniel took her hand and pressed a kiss to the backs of her fingers, and she cursed her foolish heart as the now familiar heat rushed into her core.

"Good morning, Christina," he murmured quietly, his eyes searching her face. "Are you well today?"

She swallowed, though her mouth had gone dry under the intensity of his gaze even as her heart broke all over again. "Yes, I am fine," she replied, softly. And physically, she was. "Although I have been rather alone this morning, which I find I do not like."

He caught her meaning, his face burning crimson as he looked away from her, releasing her hand. Clearing his throat, he gestured for Lord Hudson to take a chair before looking back at them both.

"Christina, I sent a message round to Lord Hudson in the early hours this morning, describing how Lord Northcliffe accosted you in the bookshop yesterday. This cannot be borne. We must do something about it."

Christina glanced at Lord Hudson, who was frowning as he poured himself a coffee.

"And what do you intend to do, Ravenhall?" Lord Hudson asked, sounding a little unconvinced. "You know how I feel regarding your plans for the man. I will not be a party to murder, and neither will your wife, I assume. If that is the action you wish to take, you are on your own."

Christina's eyes widened as she turned to look at her husband, who was shooting a rather frustrated glance toward Lord Hudson.

"I made a promise to each of you that before I undertake any rash actions, we must determine the man's guilt. Following that... well, I have no intention of striking the man down in broad daylight, for I do not fancy the noose. However, something must be done."

"And what is that to be?" Christina asked, raising an eyebrow. No matter what Daniel felt was necessary, if he murdered the man, his soul would only grow blacker, and there would be no chance of rescuing him from the depths of depravity. "Do you have a plan for how to ascertain his guilt?"

Christina saw Daniel clear his throat and sit up a little taller, as though he had come up with a marvelous idea.

"We will make him confess."

Closing her eyes, disappointment crashed through Christina. That was not a plan which had any substance, not when Lord Northcliffe had been so careful not to say a word to anyone for so many years. There was no chance that Lord Northcliffe would confess a word.

"And how will you do that, Daniel?" Lord Hudson asked, refilling Christina's cup of tea, and she accepted it gratefully as it seemed she had forgotten to place hostess and it was all she could stomach at the moment. "The man is hardly likely to say anything of importance to anyone, and the authorities will need credible witnesses before they will do anything about it. Even then, it will be difficult to have anything done about the matter, though you are fortunate your father holds great power."

Daniel shrugged. "We will need to devise a plan," he said. "Though I am thinking perhaps it may be best to take this into my own hands. My first idea is to slit his throat in the dead of night."

Christina dropped her teaspoon with a clatter, breathing hard as a vision of blood splattering across Daniel's face tore at her mind.

"He will not do anything of the sort, Christina," Lord Hudson interrupted, calmly, frowning heavily at Daniel. "Will you, Ravenhall? But yes, you are correct to say that we do need to think of something. You have been chasing Lord Northcliffe for years, and I think if you are to have anything close to a happy future, you will need to remove him from your life for good."

"He needs to be found guilty over Laura's death,"

Christina said, slowly, watching as her husband turned to face her. "That is the only way you can ever leave this to rest, is it not?"

Daniel nodded, though he looked somewhat contemplative, and Christina worried over whether he needed to see Lord Northcliffe guilty or whether he would need more than that. Her fears remained high that he would kill the man and spend the rest of his life consumed by his actions. "I am glad you understand, Christina."

There was no tenderness in his voice, no gentle smile on his face or warmth in his eyes as he spoke but rather just a firm practicality that made her want to weep.

"Then what do we think we can do?" Lord Hudson asked, shooting her a sympathetic look as though he understood the difficulty she was facing with her husband. "How do we get a man so determined to remain silent on the matter of Miss Churston's death to reveal himself to a group of witnesses? It is quite impossible."

Daniel nodded slowly, his gaze resting on Christina for a moment before he looked away. "There are ways to make a man talk," he said with determination. "Lord Northcliffe cannot continue to infiltrate my life, nor be allowed to intimidate Christina just because he feels as though he has the power to do so."

Christina could not think, her mind too full of what had occurred between them last night and his return to his prior self this morning. Her head began to ache and she rubbed it ineffectually.

"I think that—" Lord Hudson was interrupted by a sudden knock at the door, which opened to reveal the butler.

"You have a note, my lord, from Mr. Stewart," said Woodward.

Christina watched as Daniel's eyes lit up, and she wished she could invoke that same reaction in him. He was more delighted by this note than by her presence, her smile, or her touch.

"Ah, look!" he exclaimed, throwing the note to Lord Hudson. "Perhaps we do not need a plan after all. Perhaps we might be able to wheedle it out of him regardless."

Lord Hudson raised one eyebrow. "So Mr. Stewart has supposedly managed to find Lord Northcliffe in an inebriated state in White's," he said, calmly. "What do you intend to do, Ravenhall?"

A slight sense of dread filling her, Christina saw her husband rise from the table at once.

"We shall go now, you and I, and you will talk to him about Laura. Drink often loosens a man's tongue, does it not?"

"I do not think this is a good idea, Daniel," Christina said slowly, aware of the frown that jumped onto her husband's face at her words as he turned to face her. "You need to think things through carefully and slowly until you arrive at a plan that is sure to work."

He shook his head impatiently. "No. Do you know how long I have been waiting for an opportunity like this? There will be a great many witnesses at White's."

"It is not as though one can nonchalantly bring up the name of a woman dead six years now. Even in a drunken state, he is unlikely to reveal anything, particularly to a friend of yours. And even if he *should* confess, and then something were to happen to him, everyone would know—"

"That is enough, Christina." Daniel's rebuke was edged with a quiet anger that made Christina smart as if he had struck her. She knew, with all of her rationality, he was being too quick, too hasty, but she could see by the resolve on his face that nothing she said would stop him. Instead, it would likely only fuel his determination to go against her wishes.

"Do not go out," he ordered her, and with all of her being

she only wished that he told her so out of a sense of worry over her wellbeing. "You will be fine here with Woodward. If Lord Northcliffe reveals his actions to us, it could be some time before anything is done about it."

Christina nodded. "Thank you for your concern, Ravenhall," she said formally, although he didn't seem to note the sarcasm in her tone. "Do send word as to what happens. And Lady Beatrice is due to come here for afternoon tea, so I have no intention of going out today."

She caught the spark of interest in Lord Hudson's eyes, and she managed a smile for him. A slight flush crept into his cheeks as he took his leave. Clearly, Beatrice had an admirer in Lord Hudson. Perhaps someone could find happiness.

"Thank you, Christina," Daniel murmured, not moving toward her to kiss her cheek or even bid her farewell. He paused after Lord Hudson exited the room, as though he wanted to say more, but then, after a moment, he simply inclined his head and shut the door behind him.

CHAPTER 19

*C*hristina spent the next hour attempting to read but found her mind unwilling to concentrate on anything other than her husband. She was uneasy with just how quickly he had left the house, how he had let his emotions overcome all reason. This desire to capture Lord Northcliffe's confession had always been there, she was sure, but for whatever reason, he had seemed almost frantic this morning. Was it because of what they had shared last night? Had the memory of Laura and her death resurfaced with such strength that he had been unable to think of anything else, nor listen to reason?

Her heart seemed to burn within her chest with pain, and she became angry with herself for feeling so much for the husband she'd never wanted in the first place. Throwing her book onto the table, she rose to her feet and began to pace up and down the library, trying desperately to get her thoughts onto something other than Daniel Harrington.

As she looked out of the window, she heard the door behind her open, and she turned around to see if a maid had appeared to take her tea tray.

To her horror, the tall, brown-haired man from the bookshop was standing in the doorway, a wide grin on his face.

"Lord Northcliffe," she breathed, her fingers scrabbling against the window sill as she fought to lean on it heavily, her body going weak with a sharp, sudden fear.

"Good morning, Christina," he said, calmly, closing the door behind him. "How lovely that we should be reacquainted so soon."

"How did you get in?"

He shrugged, his eyes roving around the room as though taking it all in. "I do not think that matters, Christina, do you? Although I will say that the staff was all *very* busy in preparing the carriage for the sudden departure of Lord Ravenhall and Lord Hudson."

Christina felt sick. Lord Northcliffe had entirely engineered this situation. He most certainly was not at White's.

"That man, Mr. Stewart, talks a lot when he is drunk," Lord Northcliffe continued, as he drew closer to her. "You cannot imagine how easy this all was."

Her skin crawled. Making sure to keep a few chairs between herself and Lord Northcliffe, Christina moved quickly toward the side of the room where the bell pull was, hoping he didn't notice her intentions.

"You can try to run from me, but I have every intention of using you for my own ends," Lord Northcliffe continued, quietly, his eyes fixed on her. "Your husband ruined my life. First, he took the woman I loved, and then he destroyed my reputation, so much so that I could hardly be seen in London any longer."

Christina stepped in front of the bell pull, keeping a large overstuffed chair between herself and Lord Northcliffe. Putting her hands behind her back, she tugged it once, twice, three times, four times, five times, while Lord Northcliffe meandered around the room, seemingly unconcerned. She had to hope that the nature of her ringing would alert the butler to the fact that something was wrong. After all, Ravenhall had mentioned to her that Woodward had been with him ever since Laura's death.

"Your husband should arrive home soon," he said, calmly, slowly making his way toward her. "I do so want him to see what is to become of you."

Christina tried not to shudder, her eyes widening as she watched him pull a pistol from his waistband. It glinted menacingly in the daylight.

"You will always be hunted," Christina replied through trembling lips, determined to keep her courage. "No matter where you go."

Lord Northcliffe chuckled darkly. "I doubt it, my dear. I will make sure your husband is suspected of your death, and his accusations against me will come to nothing. He will look the fool. There will be no one with any reason to chase me. And, if something goes wrong, well, I have a remote place in Scotland where no one will find me."

For a moment, Christina wondered why the man was telling her all this, only to realize that he did not care for he intended to kill her before she could say a word. A cold sheen of sweat broke out over her brow, and she clung to the back of the chair, her eyes flicking wildly around the room as she desperately sought a way to escape him.

"Lord Ravenhall does not deserve to be happy," Lord Northcliffe continued, as Christina struggled to come up with any kind of solution. "He took Laura away from me, and so I have decided he is to live alone, without hope, for the rest of his days — as I have."

"Why did you do it?" Christina asked, desperately, trying to keep him talking, to allow enough time for Daniel to return.

"Do what?" he asked, arching an eyebrow.

"K-kill her," she choked out. "If you loved her so much, why couldn't you simply allow her to be happy?"

"Oh, Lady Ravenhall," Northcliffe chuckled in such a sinister way that chills fell down Christina's spine. "Is that what he has told you, what he has made you believe?"

Goose flesh rose on her arms as he stared at her and shook his head as if in sympathy.

"*I* never killed Laura Churston," he said with enough sorrow that Christina nearly believed him. "No, Laura had gone to Ravenhall's home to tell him how she truly felt — that she still loved me. We were to run off together, to find our way to Scotland and elope. Her father much preferred that she marry the son of a duke, but we were in love. She clearly told Ravenhall and he killed her for it. Apparently, if *he* couldn't have her, then neither could I."

Christina could barely process his words. *No.* She shook her head as she stared at him, her body growing cold and freezing in place at the smug smile of satisfaction that clung to his lips.

"I don't believe you," she whispered, but even she could hear the lack of conviction in her words.

"Come, my dear Christina, are you not aware of your husband's actions? He won't hesitate to take a life if necessary. He had no qualms with Miss Churston. Now we will see how he feels to have his wife taken from him."

Out of the corner of her eye, Christina saw the door handle turn very slowly, and relief washed through her. Perhaps her frantic bell pulling had done what she'd intended.

Hoping to draw his attention, Christina gave a harsh laugh, seeing Lord Northcliffe stare at her as though she'd gone mad.

"Do you truly believe that I make Lord Ravenhall happy?"

she asked in a loud voice, gesturing wildly to keep his attention focused solely on her. "It was an arrangement, nothing more. We are not even friends, Lord Northcliffe. Truly, to kill me would be to end what has been nothing more than a nightmare."

Lord Northcliffe lifted one eyebrow, his eyes still fixed on her. "Is that so?" he murmured, as the door opened a little more. "Regardless of that, Lady Ravenhall, I'm afraid that I will still put my plan into action."

Christina saw the door fly open at that, and Daniel stepped inside with Lord Hudson remaining by the door. Lord Northcliffe threw himself toward her. Stretching his arm out, he grabbed Christina and ground the pistol into her temple. Her heart began to pound wildly, and she struggled to breathe. Black spots seemed to cloud her vision as she saw her life hanging in the balance.

"Move and I'll shoot her," Lord Northcliffe said, slowly. "You're a little earlier than I expected, Ravenhall — and you brought Hudson with you. How wonderful."

"Put the pistol down," Daniel grated, his eyes fixed on Lord Northcliffe, even though Christina was desperate for him to look at her.

Lord Northcliffe chuckled, shaking his head. "So it appears I shall have to go on the run after all," he murmured, his gaze settling on Christina. "I am sure you will understand, my dear, for I cannot remain in London with two bodies by my feet, although I fully intend to leave your husband alive, to know what it is like to live alone as I do. Unfortunately, I only have two pistols, so Lord Ravenhall and I will have to fight it out to the death with our swords, unless he is too overcome by the death of his wife and his friend which, I hope, will play out to my advantage."

Christina struggled to breathe, her whole body shaking

terribly as she continued to look down the barrel of the gun. One shot. One shot that would end her life and bring about the start of Daniel's destruction. She did not think that he could cope should Lord Northcliffe continue to haunt him. For he must be lying — Daniel couldn't have killed Miss Churston... could he have?

Slowly, her gaze traveled back toward Daniel, and Christina found herself aching for all of the space between them. She didn't know what to believe of him. Perhaps, had she been truly honest with him, had she bared her soul and trusted him, he might have returned some feeling toward her. For despite Lord Northcliffe's words, despite what she knew of Daniel's past actions, as she looked at the despair that had come over his face, she realized that he could never have hurt an innocent woman, no matter what she had done to him.

Finally, he looked back at her, his gaze remaining steady although his eyes held a hint of fear.

"Daniel," she called out. "This isn't your fault. And... and this isn't a nightmare, you know that. There is more between us that I only wish we had the opportunity to explore."

A tear leaked from her eye, but she continued to watch Daniel, holding onto his gaze as it was the only thing that mattered.

"You don't deserve any of this," she heard Lord Northcliffe say, his voice now thin and filled with rage. "You took away my love from me, and now it will bring me the greatest of pleasures to do the same to you."

As his attention moved toward Daniel, the pistol moved a fraction of an inch away from her temple, and Christina took the moment of opportunity to do the only thing she could think of.

She collapsed onto the floor, just as the sound of a pistol shot reached her ears. There was no pain, no scream of injury. Instead, there was the sound of splintering wood, of running feet and shouting voices.

And then there were strong hands reaching for her, helping her to sit up. Dazed, Christina recognized that her husband was the one holding her.

"Daniel!" she breathed, closing her eyes as tears began to pour into her vision. "You're safe."

"As are you," he murmured, pulling her into his arms. "Thank goodness you are all right. For a moment there I thought I would lose you."

Movement at the door caught her eye, and Christina watched as Lord Hudson attempted to block the exit. It was at that moment, however, she heard a voice that made her cringe. Christina had completely forgotten about Beatrice's visit, and her timing could not have been worse.

"Christina? Are you here?" came Beatrice's melodic voice from outside of the hallway. "The door was ajar and no servants were in sight, so I let myself in." She walked through the doorway, just as Christina began to call out to her to stay back. "Are you well to—oh!"

She came to a halt, her eyes wide as she surveyed the scene in front of her. Lord Northcliffe pulled a second pistol from his waistband, pointing it at Beatrice, and despair coursed through Christina. *Do not let Beatrice be hurt by this*, she prayed.

"Lady Beatrice!" Lord Hudson said desperately — too desperately, it seemed, as Lord Northcliffe looked from him to Beatrice with a gleam in his eye.

"Out of my way, Hudson, or say farewell to the woman here."

Christina could see the dismay on the face of Lord Hudson, but he could do nothing except step out of the way. As Lord Northcliffe rushed out of the room, Lord Hudson put his arms on Beatrice's shoulders, saying something softly to her, before rushing out after Lord Northcliffe.

Christina felt completely helpless, but for the moment, she focused on Daniel's presence. Lord Hudson would catch him, she told herself. He had to — for until he was caught, this ordeal would never be over.

CHAPTER 20

"We've found him."

Daniel spun around on hearing Hudson's voice, staring at his friend for a moment before letting out a sigh of relief. It had been a couple of hours since he'd left, chasing after Northcliffe.

"He's meant to be on his way to Scotland, but he's holed up in some inn just outside of London," Hudson continued, coming a little farther into the room and making his way straight toward the brandy tray. "Whoever or whatever he's waiting for hasn't shown up, and my guess is he cannot carry on without it."

Daniel's heart jumped with exaltation as the urge to go straight to wherever Northcliffe was hiding pushed him into action.

"He should never have been able to escape in the first place," he said, as Hudson handed him a brandy. "However, Lady Beatrice—"

"Had she not arrived when she did, perhaps this would all be over," Daniel said with some bitterness in his voice.

Hudson faced him with consternation on his face. "Or,

perhaps, *I* would have been over. Had Lady Beatrice not distracted Northcliffe, you could have been attending my funeral." He took a sip of his drink. "It's just as well we have a few men on hand. They've been following him since he left the house. It means we can do this properly."

But I don't want to do this properly.

That was the problem that now faced Daniel. He had no intention of handing Northcliffe into the authorities, not now. Not when the man had been so close to robbing him of his wife. No, if he found Northcliffe, it would be to end his life in the same way he'd tried to end Christina's.

"Is something wrong, Ravenhall?"

Daniel shook his head. "No."

"Are you sure?"

Aware that his friend knew him well, Daniel drew in a long breath and took a hearty sip of his brandy before replying.

"Hudson, Northcliffe went too far this time," he said, eventually. "I do not intend to allow the man to live."

Hudson's eyes narrowed.

"For heaven's sake, he was about to murder Christina!" Daniel exclaimed upon Lord Hudson's grimace. "That would be the second love he'd have taken away from me!"

Lord Hudson raised one eyebrow, a slow smile spreading across his face as the words Daniel had spoken seemed to echo around the room. Daniel's cheeks warmed as he not only realized what he'd had said but also that it was too late to take it back.

"My, my," Hudson murmured softly. "So this is it, is it? How interesting. You can finally admit you care for your wife."

"No," Daniel said, brusquely, turning away from his friend. "No, not in that way."

"Ravenhall," came Hudson's reply. "You are allowed to be

in love with your wife, as I am sure I have said to you before. Why do you insist on pushing her away? You have already admitted it to me. You cannot continue to ignore such a depth of feeling."

Releasing a long breath, Daniel set down his brandy glass and leaned on his study table, looking down at the sheaf of paper there. He did not see anything but Christina's face, caught up as he was in the memory of how she'd looked when he'd seen her with Northcliffe.

His heart had torn open, becoming a yawning chasm that he could not ignore. It was an abyss he had not filled in years, choosing to descend into darkness and to ignore the happiness another might bring.

He had not looked at any other lady since Laura, had only married because he had been forced into the match. But on seeing Christina so afraid, so close to a tragedy, he had felt his heart break free of the chains he'd placed around it.

He loved his wife.

"Ravenhall, I must consider this a good thing," Hudson continued when he didn't say anything. "Do not turn away from it now. Allow yourself to love her without feeling any of the guilt I know you have burdened yourself with for too long."

Daniel frowned, opening his mouth to refute his friend's statement but finding he could not do so.

The truth was, he did feel guilty about forgetting Laura. That was why he had left Christina's bed after giving himself to her so completely. He could not even recall Laura's face, could not remember the feeling that he'd always considered to be so overwhelming when her memory had come to mind. The feelings he had for Christina — well, they were stronger than any he had ever known before, and that created a guilt that tore at his soul.

"I should not be so forgetful," he grated, his head now hanging low.

"She is gone and you need to let her go," Lord Hudson replied, his voice firm. "You have dwelt on this for years, Ravenhall, but instead of finding healing, you have allowed it to build guilt and pain and sorrow within you. Now Christina has come into your life, and you refuse to give her the one thing she wants because your guilt will not allow you to do so." Daniel looked up and caught Hudson smiling gently. "I know she cares for you, Ravenhall. You are in doubt about that yourself, I think. If you leave Laura in the past, no one will condemn you. It is only you who stands in judgment upon yourself, as foolish as that sounds. Leave the past in the past and focus on the future."

"On Christina," Daniel breathed, nodding slowly as he walked around the table and sat down in an overstuffed chair, facing the fire.

"Yes," Hudson chuckled, his smile broadening. "On Christina. Goodness knows you have both been through more than enough to look forward to a bit of a quiet life."

That did not bring a smile to Daniel's face. He could not have a quiet life, as Hudson put it, not when Northcliffe remained a threat.

"I mean to mete out punishment, Hudson," he said, firmly. "When we find Northcliffe, he will receive no mercy from me. The man deserves to die."

Hudson raised his eyebrows. "That is not what I expected to hear from you. This morning, you were speaking of a plan to make him confess. You know the views of your wife — how will she feel if she knows what you have done?"

Daniel shook his head. "My plan was formed before he entered my home and tried to kill Christina. I will punish him for what he did and what he tried to do. There are consequences he must face."

"And you think you are the one to bring him down to the grave?" Lord Hudson asked, calmly.

Daniel shook his head. "For once, I shall be the executioner. That is all."

A quiet knock came to the door of his study and, before he could call out, it opened and in stepped Christina.

She was looking rather tired and pale; instead, her eyes were bright and there was no longer any trembling in her limbs.

"Christina," Daniel said at once, getting to his feet and hurrying over to her. "You should be resting."

"I am quite well, I thank you," she replied, with a soft edge of steel to her voice. "The maid told me of Lord Hudson's arrival, and I had to know what had been done."

Daniel offered her his arm, and a tremble shot through him as she took it, though she kept her gaze ahead of her and not upon his face.

Goodness, she took his breath away. He couldn't quite say why. Perhaps it was her quiet poise, or maybe her quaint, oft-overlooked charm. Whatever it was, she calmed a peace of his soul that he hadn't known was possible to regain.

"Have you made any progress, Lord Hudson?" she asked, as Daniel seated her by the fire. "Have you found Lord Northcliffe?"

Hudson cleared his throat and rose from his chair in the corner of the room to draw closer to Christina. "Yes. We have. It appears the men we use to help us find those who require our help are also rather good at following a criminal."

Daniel watched Christina closely, seeing how she swallowed hard and nodded, her hands tightening together as she held them in her lap.

She was more affected than she wanted them to see.

"You need not fear anymore, Christina," he said, softly,

reaching for her hand and holding it tightly in his own. "We are to set out for him once it is dark."

Her eyes caught his, confused. "Dark?"

He nodded. "Northcliffe is at an inn only two hours' ride from London," he explained. "We think he is to go to Scotland but something has held him up. The road will be well lit by the full moon, and so we shall go under cover of night to take him by surprise."

She held his gaze for a moment, and Daniel's breath caught in his chest at the deep emotions in her eyes, though her look was troubled.

"I haven't told you everything that Lord Northcliffe said to me," she said, in a somewhat tremulous voice. "He told me that if he had to, he would go to Scotland, to hide there so that he could not easily be found or convicted."

Daniel listened with growing anger as Christina recounted the words Lord Northcliffe had said to her. The arrogant fool had apparently believed he would be able to kill Christina and leave her body for Daniel to find, and seemed to have told her everything, believing she would never have the chance to speak the truth aloud.

"There is something else," she said, and he noted the way she twisted her fingers in her lap. "He was quite adamant about the fact that he wanted to kill me because you had taken Miss Churston from him, Daniel. Not that you had taken her love, but rather, he clearly believed that *you* were the one who killed her."

The room went completely silent for a moment as Daniel took in her words. He clenched his fists in anger that Northcliffe had not only sought to take Christina from him but had attempted to turn her against him in the process.

"Do you believe him?" he finally asked, and when she raised her head to look at him, he saw the turmoil in her face.

"No," she said, though her words lacked conviction.

His heart fell as anguish washed over him.

"No," she repeated with more determination, peering into his face; he must have worn the question in his expression. "I do not believe you would take the life of an innocent woman," she said firmly.

"But?"

"But I did believe him when he said he didn't kill her," she said softly. "He told me she had arrived at your home to tell you that she was running off with him to be married. He said..." She hesitated, as if not wanting to share anything further with him.

"What did he say, Christina?" he demanded, rather than asked.

"He said that she only agreed to marry you because her father had learned of your affection for her and much preferred that she marry a future duke. That she still loved Northcliffe and they had a plan to be together. She came to your townhouse that night to tell you of this."

Daniel rose to his feet and began to pace the room, unable to meet the sympathetic gazes of Lord Hudson and Christina. He wanted to deny all that she said, to tell her Northcliffe had simply been playing with her emotions, been turning her against him. And yet, as much turmoil as he felt, he began to review the logic of what she said. He thought back to his relationship with Laura, to the times they had together. She always had a quiet demeanor, a gentleness he found endearing. But what had he really known of her? For all these years, he had thought he loved her and she him in turn, but when he recalled the times they had run into Lord Northcliffe, he remembered the warm smile that had crossed her face, the jealousy that had tugged at his heart. Was there something more there, something he had missed, that perhaps he hadn't wanted to see?

"I'm sorry, Daniel," Christina said in almost a whisper. "I know not what to say, what to believe—"

"You would believe him, a man you hardly know, who threatened to kill you, over your own husband?" he seethed, allowing the more familiar anger to overcome him. All else he thought and felt shriveled in the face of fresh hurt now that he had recognized his deep feelings toward her. She put a hand on his arm, and he shook it off in disgust. "Come, Hudson, it is time we go. Christina, we will be returning to London shortly, though Lord Northcliffe will not."

Her eyes widened. "What do you mean?"

"I mean, I have no intention of letting the man go," he said, calmly and reasonably. "After what he did to Laura and what he was about to do to you, I cannot let him live."

Christina stared at him for a long moment, her eyes filling with tears. "No, Daniel," she said, her voice quiet and filled with horror. "If you do such a thing, it will haunt you forever."

"So be it," he said, filled with a determination to do just that. "I am the one he has injured. I am the one he chose to attack. I should, therefore, be the one to bring an end to all of this."

She shook her head, and one of the tears pooling in her eyes spilled over and flowed down her cheek.

He grieved the loss of her affection toward him, her belief in him, and his heart ached with a sudden, furious pain. How could she not see what he had to do? That he had to be the one to bring an end to the agony he'd been forced to endure these last few years, that he could never move forward until he had done so?

"Do not ask me to step away from this," he said, haltingly. "I cannot do that, Christina. I must bring Northcliffe's last judgment upon him."

She looked back at him steadily, her tears gone as her lips

drew into a long, thin line. "And who made you judge and jury?" she asked, firmly. "Who brought you out as executioner? You have suffered, yes, but you are better than him, Daniel. You are not like Lord Northcliffe in any way!"

Daniel curled his hand into a fist, the fingernails biting into the soft skin of his palm. "I must do this."

"No," she said, getting up from her chair in a flurry of skirts. "No, you are *choosing* to take on a role you have no right to bear. This pain will never lift, not if you kill the man responsible. Not if you become what he is."

"She is right," Hudson murmured, lifting one eyebrow.

Daniel clenched his jaw.

"You cannot let him do this, Hudson!" Christina exclaimed, holding her hands up in a gesture of helplessness. "How can you let him go when you know what he will do?"

Hudson gave her a sad smile. "Because I must. I swore to help him find the man, and so I will. What he does once he finds him is his responsibility." He turned his gaze toward Daniel, shaking his head. "Although I confess I miss the man I once knew all those years ago. I have stayed by your side, Daniel, and I have seen the pain you have carried for as many years, but I no longer know this man standing in front of me."

"Then you are right. You do not know me. For I am *exactly* that kind of man!" Daniel threw from his chair. "I am the kind of man who wants restitution for what he has suffered! I am the kind of man who seeks justice for the crimes committed against him! I am the kind of man who wants to, finally, put this to rest."

His words echoed around the room, bouncing off the walls as he struggled to draw in a breath, his anger burning so hotly he feared he could not contain it.

"Then I will not be here when you return," Christina said, her quiet voice drawing his attention and bringing his anger down to nothing more than a sputtering flame. "I love you, Daniel, I do, but I cannot accept this, not when there is another way. I will not be present when the authorities come for you, when they arrest you for killing another man in cold blood."

He laughed at her, his frustration covering the pain that coursed through him over the fact she would not accept him if he followed through with what he must do, despite his love for her. "I am a marquess, Christina, a future duke. Should they come for me, then I will explain all to them. I will tell them exactly what he did to me, to my first love, and then to my wife. I shall not be held."

"Daniel…" she said softly, her eyes sparkling with tears. "If you are set free, you will simply live in an imprisonment of your own doing, of knowing who you have become."

Daniel did not say anything, his words turning to sand as she stepped past him, her fingers brushing his hand as she passed.

"Goodbye, Daniel," she murmured, one hand on the door handle as she looked back at him. "I shall have my things sent to your country estate tonight and will follow shortly if needed. I shall go to my father's townhouse for the evening and pray fervently that you will not do this reckless act." She gave him a small smile, just as a single tear trickled down her cheek. "I will pray that you will prove yourself to be a better man than that. That you will be the man I know you can be, not the one who throws all he has away simply to bring a veil of justice over all that he has experienced."

Tears fell from her eyes like rain as she watched him, her smile remaining steady regardless. "Be the man I love. The one I can trust."

The door closed behind her, and Daniel felt his heart go with her, leaving an empty shadow of a man behind.

CHAPTER 21

aniel leaped from his mount's back before the creature came to a complete halt, tossing the reins to the stablehand who was hiding a yawn behind his loosely clenched fist. Daniel did not care about the hour, not when he could finally get his hands on Northcliffe.

"Ravenhall," Hudson called out firmly. From behind him "Hold for a moment."

Daniel drew in a long breath and turned around just as his friend dismounted behind him.

"This is as far as I will come," Hudson said, as the stable-hand took the second horse. "I will come into the inn to guard the door, but I will not be part of the rest."

Daniel stared at his friend for a moment, seeing the steadiness of Hudson's gaze.

"You are quite serious!" he exclaimed, completely taken aback. "But why, Hudson? I know you disapprove of my plan but—"

Hudson nodded. "That is it precisely."

"Then why help me at all?"

"Because I promised I would," came the calm reply. "I

always said that I would help you find the man responsible. Even though the authorities had nothing to hold him on, I had always presumed that we would mete out justice in a less murderous way."

Daniel let out a long, frustrated breath. "I am not murderous, Hudson."

Hudson snorted. "Yes, you are. Perhaps you could take this gentleman down through taking away his finances, by finding a way to discredit him, by forcing him to live quietly without all the things he so clearly loves in society? You said yourself you wanted to find a way to make the man confess before handing him to the authorities."

He shrugged, helplessly, before continuing. "I have seen what you have done in the past, Ravenhall, but I thought that Christina's words and her very presence in your life would bring some sense to your troubled heart, that reason would enter your scope of view, but it seems I was mistaken."

He reached forward and put one firm hand on Daniel's shoulder. "I cannot go with you any farther. Whatever you do, you will do it without a witness. I have my own plans for my future, and I cannot allow this to affect them."

"Your own future?" Daniel repeated, a little surprised. "You have never spoken of such things before."

"That is because I have never been serious about a lady before," Hudson replied, frankly. "Lady Beatrice shall be my bride if I can persuade her and, since I shall have no requirement to help you in your search for Lord Northcliffe any longer, I intend to focus my time on her. Not that I plan to drop the work you started in aiding others, but I have my own happiness to think of now."

For a moment, Daniel was stunned. It sounded as though Hudson was almost resentful of him, as though his friend were frustrated that their search was to come to such an end.

"You don't understand," he said, hoarsely. "I must do this."

"No," Lord Hudson replied, his voice firm. "You are choosing to do this. And the consequences of which will not only affect you but will also affect your wife, the woman you have only just declared yourself to love, whom you have yet to inform of the fact." He shrugged, gesturing toward the inn. "But this is your own decision."

Daniel lifted his chin, choosing to stride forward and away from Hudson. He did not look back at his friend, even though he felt his presence behind him. His heart began to quicken wildly in his chest as he opened the door to the inn. Only a few drunken patrons sat at the tables while the innkeeper glowered at him from behind the counter.

As he walked toward the innkeeper, Daniel's body coiled with tension. He was only a short distance away from his quarry. Somewhere near, Northcliffe was waiting.

"I need to speak with a gentleman who came here earlier today," he said, pulling out a sheaf of notes from his pocket. "I will make it worth your while not to notice my presence here."

The innkeeper's glower disappeared. "Of course," he murmured, taking the money. "You'll be looking for a fine gentleman, then?"

"Yes."

The innkeeper rubbed his chin. "Only got one of them here this evening. A Lord Norcourt, I believe."

The name did not disconcert Daniel. It was not as though Northcliffe would give the man his real name. "And where might he be?"

"Upstairs," the innkeeper replied, jerking his head toward the narrow staircase. "The last door on your left." His sharp eyes turned back toward Daniel. "Although I'd guess the door will be good and bolted."

Daniel frowned. "Then is there a key?"

The innkeeper raised one eyebrow, chuckling when Daniel sighed and pulled out a few coins.

"Very good, my lord," he grinned, pocketing the lot. "Here's the key. I won't say nothing."

Daniel took the solid key in his hand and looked down at it for a moment, his breath quickening.

"Thank you," he said, firmly. "I'll be sure to return it."

The innkeeper shrugged, turning away from him. "Just leave it in the lock. The less I see of you the better."

At least we agree about that, Daniel thought, as he turned back to the staircase, making sure to ignore Hudson, who was now leaning against the wall by the front door. He did not want to look at his friend for fear that his resolve would die out, the heaviness in his heart growing all the more as he climbed each step.

This was not what he'd thought he would feel like, knowing that Northcliffe was only a few meters away. Daniel had believed he would be exuberant, filled with energy and a deep focus but, instead, his heart was heavy with a growing weight of guilt.

Christina came to his mind, her eyes sparkling with tears as she looked at him, and Daniel was forced to catch his breath, leaning on the rail. It was as though she was right there with him, urging him not to do what he intended.

"I have to," he muttered out loud, as though speaking to her, and he forced one foot in front of the other. "I have to do this. It's the only way."

Locating the last door on the left, Daniel paused for a moment to steady his breath, closing his eyes tightly. Slowly putting the key in the lock in an attempt to make as little noise as possible, he turned it carefully, wincing as it squeaked.

Then, with as much strength as he could, he flung the

door open and stormed inside, one hand pulling the pistol from his belt.

"Northcliffe!" he shouted, as the man jumped from his chair, scrambling backward in shock. "You're not going to be able to escape this time."

There was nothing but fear and resentment in Northcliffe's eyes. Gone was the mocking smile, the confident gaze, the grin of delight over Daniel's upset. Instead, the man appeared weak, thin, and afraid.

It bolstered Daniel's courage.

Smirking, Daniel closed the door behind him and leaned against it for a moment. Northcliffe's eyes darted about the room.

"There's no escape, I'm afraid," Daniel said slowly, spotting the window and knowing that the man wouldn't jump to the ground for fear of death. "You're not going anywhere. Not to Scotland, like you'd planned."

Northcliffe's lip curled.

"That wife of yours was never meant to survive," he grated, a flicker of determination returning to his gaze. "I thought I'd shot her."

"You didn't," Daniel replied, calmly, waving his pistol at Northcliffe. "She is very much alive and told me everything. She was witness to your confession. There's nothing left for you now."

Northcliffe's eyes glittered. "And so you've come to kill me, is that it?"

Daniel shrugged. "Perhaps." It wasn't what he'd been intending to say, but then again, he'd not been quite certain how he'd react when faced with this man again.

"Then do it," Northcliffe replied, sitting down on the bed and looking directly at Daniel, challenging him. "It's the easiest way out of all this, after all. I have nothing to live for any longer."

His words struck hard against Daniel's mind, like hammer blows that thundered in his head. By doing this, by taking Lord Northcliffe's life in a quiet inn with no one about, it was the easiest way for Northcliffe to receive what was due him. No one would ever know. He could be free of Northcliffe, free of his past. And yet...

Suddenly, his determination to shoot the man faltered. Christina's words came back to his mind, burning a path into his heart. She believed he wasn't this kind of man, not the kind of man who became a vengeful murderer. And yet, here he stood with a pistol in his hand, determined to do just that.

Daniel found himself growing desperate to prove to Christina that he could be the man she wanted him to be. That he could be trusted, even when faced with the opportunity to kill the man who'd caused him so much pain.

"I want to kill you," he said slowly, still keeping his pistol steady. "You deserve to die. But this is too easy for you, Northcliffe. The world deserves to know the truth about Laura. That is one way I can bring her and her family justice."

Northcliffe's expression twisted, grew ugly. "You're weak," he spat, getting to his feet. "You've always been weak. Too weak to do what you'd planned, to do what you want instead of listening to that stupid lady you call a wife. It's her that makes you this way."

It was as though, instead of tormenting him all the more, Northcliffe's words revealed a strange truth to Daniel. It was not that Christina made him weak but rather that she was giving him the strength *not* to do what he'd come here to do. Her voice, her smile, the light in her eyes all came back to him, flooding his memory. The look on her face as she'd told him she was leaving tore at his mind, and he knew that right here, in this little room, was the moment he had to make a decision that would change the course of the rest of his life.

He could exact his revenge on Lord Northcliffe, just as

he'd intended, and leave him dead at his feet. That would mean estrangement from Christina, very little chance to give expression to his growing feelings for her and, most likely, a lifetime spent alone, in the darkness that had become familiar.

If he did not kill Lord Northcliffe, then his future would look very different. Christina would have no cause to doubt him, would come back to live with him as she should and he would have nothing to fear from any authorities. Northcliffe would be subsequently dealt with in the official manner which, while it could take a little longer, would give Daniel the chance to see his first love avenged in the way that was right. It would not be by his hand, but it would be his voice giving evidence, as well as that of Christina and Hudson.

I love her. As she does me.

The voice whispered in his mind as he slowly lowered the pistol, his heart swelling with an as-yet unspoken emotion. "Northcliffe," he said, firmly, never taking his gaze away from the man. "You're coming with me."

Lord Northcliffe spat, hard. "No, I'm not. Kill me now. Let this whole thing be over with. Kill me as you did Laura."

Daniel gave a grunt of frustration.

"What do you mean, as I killed Laura? There is no one here, Northcliffe, so you may as well confess all. You know as well as I do that it was you who killed her and left her for me to find. Why lie about it now?"

Daniel, his jaw hard, leaned a little closer to the man.

"If you're afraid of the gallows, Northcliffe, then—"

Northcliffe's eyes widened as he stared at him, and he surprised Daniel by raising his hands in front of him, as if in surrender.

"You didn't do it." Northcliffe said softly, to himself, it seemed, as much as Daniel.

"Didn't do what? Kill Laura? Of course not, you fool, I—"

Their gazes met, and suddenly they both came to the realization at the same time. Despite how they hated one another and their irreparable past, they both knew at that moment that neither one of them had killed Laura Churston.

"So who did it?" Daniel said hoarsely, gripping a chair beside him as his legs suddenly grew weak. "Who else would have a wish to harm her? And why would my butler say— my God."

Desperation flooded over him as he grasped the man's collar, lifting him and pushing him toward the door. "We have to go — *now*. Lord Hudson is waiting."

Northcliffe walked down the long flight of stairs with Daniel following close behind. Outside, Hudson raised his eyebrows in astonishment as he pushed himself away from the wall.

"Hudson, I have no time to explain," he said in a rush. "Northcliffe did not kill Laura, though he did still threaten Christina's life. I have to go. Christina is in danger."

"But—"

"I believe Woodward is somehow involved," he said as Hudson stood in attention with an astonished gaze at his words. Daniel pushed Lord Northcliffe toward him. "I cannot say I completely trust you, Northcliffe, so Lord Hudson will accompany you for now," he continued, throwing a nod of appreciation toward the innkeeper who returned his gesture. "Is there a carriage of some sort?"

"I'm sure we can procure one, despite the hour," Lord Hudson replied, still keeping a firm hold of Lord Northcliffe. "Well done, old boy. Didn't think you had it in you."

"Neither did I," Daniel admitted. "It seems Christina has had more of an influence on me than she realized." He drew a resolute breath. "This is not over yet."

Lord Hudson threw him a glance, which Daniel only just caught in the dim light.

"I must go. I will see you in London," he said, leaving Hudson behind and making for the stables as quickly as possible. He found his mount, yelling at a confused stable-hand to saddle him — quickly. Daniel threw a leg overtop the horse, and raced out of the stables already at a gallop. He prayed Christina was, by now, safely residing with her father. He could not wait to tell her the truth, to show her that all of his trials had finally come to an end. Suddenly his future was brighter than ever before, a lightness he had not experienced in a great many years settling over him. But first, he had to ensure her safety. All should be fine, he assured himself. Woodward had no reason to do her harm — did he?

"I can let you go now, Laura," he said softly as he rode. "You will have the justice that should always have been yours."

Looking up at the full moon, Daniel closed his eyes for a moment and drew in a long, ragged breath. The burden he'd been carrying for so long had finally gone, rolling away from his back the moment he'd chosen not to kill Lord North-cliffe. He knew now that Northcliffe hadn't been the killer, and yet, even though he still had to make certain Woodward was dealt with, Daniel felt his spirit lift at the fact that he had let go of the thirst for vengeance that had been a part of him for so long. He let out a breath and opened his eyes. It no longer mattered that he could not recall Laura's face, nor the sound of her voice. She was gone to a place he could not follow, and in spite of his brokenness, in spite of his grief, he had found another to love. Christina was his everything; he had just never allowed himself to feel it before.

"I love her," he breathed, urging his horse to travel faster. "I love my wife." Saying the words were more freeing than anything else he could ever have imagined. Now he had to make sure he had the opportunity to tell her.

CHAPTER 22

*C*hristina did not sleep well that night. She'd had every intention of returning to her father's home for a time before removing to her husband's country estate, only to find upon arriving that her father was no longer in London. The note had been returned to her by the butler, who informed her that the Marquess of Burrton had apparently gone to a house party in Suffolk and would not return for another sennight.

And so, Christina had no other option but to remain in her home, waiting for her husband to return or for the authorities to come to the door with the news that Daniel had been arrested for murder — despite the fact that, as he had said, he was a powerful marquess.

Her heart broke as she thought of what he intended to do, and she prayed over and over that he would find the strength to do what was right, while fully believing that he would not be able to. She had seen the anger in his eyes as he'd spoken of Lord Northcliffe, reminding her of how she'd almost been killed by the man.

And while that had been a terrifying experience, Christina did not want Daniel to throw the rest of his life away by taking another man's life from him. While Lord Northcliffe clearly had an evil heart and venomous intentions toward Daniel, Christina could not justify her husband killing the man instead of taking him to the authorities. What Lord Northcliffe had said to her still made her rather uneasy. There was every possibility that he was trying to create distance between her and Daniel, and yet she had a nagging sense that he was being truthful — that he hadn't been the one to kill Miss Churston. In the same breath, she refused to believe Daniel had killed her either. But who was to blame?

Sighing, Christina pushed herself away from the dining table, as she had found herself picking at her toast, the only thing she could currently stomach. Wandering to the window, she looked out at the street below, her heart growing heavier with every second that passed. Daniel and Lord Hudson had not yet returned, and it was agony not knowing where they had gone or what they were doing. Her mind filled with visions of what might have happened to her husband — could he be injured, bloodied, or even killed? Had Lord Northcliffe been waiting for them? Had he known Daniel would pursue him? Perhaps the man had organized some kind of ambush, and Daniel and Hudson would never return home at all.

A small sob escaped her. This was not what she had hoped for when she'd agreed to marry him.

"My lady?"

Turning around, Christina wiped her eyes as the butler came into the room, a small sympathetic smile on his face.

"You need not fear any longer, my lady. Lord Ravenhall has just written a note on the chance you were still at home. Here."

Christina grasped it with trembling fingers, opening it at once.

"We are safe," she read aloud, sinking down slowly into a seat. Christina realized it was the first time Daniel had ever written anything to her. Funny, she had thought his writing would be heavy and bold, whereas this seemed to be hurriedly scratched. He must have been in a rush. "All is well and has been dealt with accordingly. Lord Northcliffe confessed to Laura's murder, and I have ensured that he will never bother us again. I shall return soon. I hope with all my heart that you will be waiting for me."

She stared at the note, reading it over and over before fixing her eyes on the butler who was standing patiently, waiting for her instruction.

"When did you say this arrived?" she asked, one hand now clinging to her chair. "Just now?"

"Yes, my lady, only a few minutes ago."

She looked at the note again, her breath coming more quickly now as the words finally registered. "Where is he?"

"The boy who delivered it said they were… taking care of things before they returned," the butler replied, though a strange look passed over his eyes. "He has done this for you, my lady."

A half-strangled sob left Christina's throat as she took in what Woodward had said. Daniel had not only killed Lord Northcliffe, but he had done it in her name. How could he, knowing how she felt?

"Shall I fetch you a fresh pot of tea, my lady?" the butler asked. "To restore you, perhaps?"

Christina could hardly breathe, her chest tightening as she gave the butler a jerky nod, though what tea would do, she wasn't sure. She could not quite believe this, having been so hopeful that Daniel would turn away from murder and find another way.

"Are you quite all right?" the butler asked hesitantly, as though a little unsure as to whether or not he should leave her side.

Christina drew in a shaking breath, the corner of her lips curving into a smile she did not feel. "Yes, of course. Thank you, Woodward. Can you have the tea tray sent to my room, please? I need to freshen up."

The butler nodded and departed, leaving Christina to make her way to her bedchamber alone. As she climbed the stairs, her steps felt as though she were walking through sand. Her words to Daniel earlier had not been an empty threat. With the cloud of murder now between them, they could never be happy together — not truly. It would only solidify his anger and hatred, and the darkness that threatened would eventually overcome him.

She would stay married to him, of course, but they would never truly be husband and wife.

The door closed with a soft thud, and Christina leaned back against it, tears threatening. But she was almost too upset to cry. Rather, she simply felt empty. She sighed as she looked across at her bed, wishing that Daniel was returning within a different set of circumstances. She so craved that connection with him again, that physical satisfaction, and yet she didn't know if she could ever be with him that way again.

It was not that Christina felt threatened by Daniel's memory of another. She knew that he would always hold Laura in his heart, but she longed for him to find room for her as well. If he could kill a man in cold blood, was he capable of true love anymore?

She looked at the adjoining door that led to his bedchamber, where she had never before ventured. She knew her own love for the wretched man, even though he had been so distant. The little she had seen of him when he had been kind and caring was the sort of man she longed to be with. Was he gone forever?

Sighing, Christina turned the door handle, thinking that he had, most likely, locked it, and was surprised to discover it open. The key tinkered quietly as it fell to the floor within the room and, as Christina opened to door to find it, she was plagued with a sudden, fierce curiosity.

She had never seen his room before, having never pried and certainly never considered that she ought to go in without his permission. Now, however, when she had the opportunity to do so and needed one last connection with her husband, Christina stepped a little farther in and looked all about her.

There was not much to see. A bed, a chair, a table by the fire, and a writing desk in the corner. A door that led to his dressing room, she assumed, was on the opposite side of the room from where she stood, but there was nothing else of particular interest. She recalled that he had not been here long, and had no plans to stay for any length of time.

Wandering into the room, Christina trailed her fingers along the row of books he had stacked neatly along one of the shelves on the wall, her heart breaking at the remembrance of just how much they both enjoyed reading. It was something she had hoped they could share more of as they spent their lives together — but it was no longer to be.

Tears burned her eyes and she fought to keep them at bay as she stumbled back to her own room. Woodward entered soon after, startling her as she had been expecting her maid.

"Woodward," she said, blinking back tears as he set the tea tray down on the small table, suddenly glad that he was here so she could make her preparations. "Will you send for my maid and ready the carriage? I must be going — and quickly, before Lord Ravenhall returns."

He looked up, concern written on his features.

"May I ask where you are going, my lady?"

"To the countryside for now," she said. "At least, until I determine what to do. It seems I... I cannot stay here any longer."

"But my lady," he said, a look of astonishment coming over his face, "Your husband will be very displeased."

"That no longer matters," she said, hearing the tension in her voice as the tears threatened to fall once more. "I cannot stay here with him any longer."

"My lord has done everything for you. He killed a man for you! The man who meant to steal his first woman away from him, and threatened your life. Why would you not be loyal to such a man?"

Christina was surprised at Woodward's sudden display of passion, but she knew the man had been with Daniel his entire life. Of course, he would be upset on his behalf.

"He well knew I never wanted it to end like that, Woodward," she said, feeling the misery deep in her soul. "His soul is blackened, and I'm not sure I can live like that. And I— Woodward, what do you mean, the man who *meant* to steal his woman?"

When Christina looked up, she was shocked at the look that had clouded his face, the wrinkled lines around his mouth and eyes hardening in anger. The circumstances surrounding Miss Churston's death sprang to her mind. *Woodward* had been the only one to claim to see Lord Northcliffe commit the murder. He had noted Northcliffe's entry and departure. Christina thought back to her conversation with Lord Northcliffe. So much was difficult to remember due to her focus on getting away from him, but he had seemed convincing when he stated that he hadn't killed Miss Churston.

She looked up at Woodward now, her astonishment overcoming all other emotion.

"Why?" she breathed. "Why did you do it? Kill an innocent woman?"

"She was no innocent," he snorted without denial.

She could hardly believe the transformation in him as he glared at her, and her heart quickened.

"Why, the woman had been spreading her legs for Northcliffe, all the while stringing along Lord Ravenhall. I have known him since he was a child, seeing him run around his father's estate. I swore my loyalty to him. My niece worked at the estate of Miss Churston's father. She heard from Miss Churston's lady's maid her plan to confess to Lord Ravenhall and then run away with Lord Northcliffe. I couldn't have it. I didn't want to see my lord thrown away like that. He is a good man, and didn't deserve to be treated with such disregard."

"So you killed her?" Christina asked, still unable to believe this elderly man, who had looked upon her with such kindness, could be a murderer.

"It was not my first kill," he said with a shrug. "I fought in the wars, found it difficult to find work when I returned. The Duke of Ware gave me my position, and I vowed undying loyalty to the family from then forward. The woman deserved it."

His look changed to one of pity and regret as he tilted his head toward Christina and sighed. "I had thought perhaps you would bring my lord happiness. But it seems you cannot accept him for who he is, and you are determined to leave him just as Miss Churston did. I tested you, my lady, and you failed."

"What are you talking about?" Christina asked, as her pulse raced wildly. Realization struck that she was in just as much danger as poor Miss Churston had been those many years ago. But she had the upper hand now, she thought. Woodward was older, and she knew his intentions, knew how he had killed the other woman. Her hands waved wildly behind her as she sought what she was looking for, trying to keep the conversation flowing as she did. "What sort of test could you set for me?"

"The note," he said with a sneer. "I wrote it, to see how you would react, to see if your love was true. And, my lady, I have found you wanting."

Woodward advanced toward her, rolling up his sleeves.

She swallowed hard and closed her fist around a candlestick.

CHAPTER 23

"Christina!" Daniel bellowed as he raced into the house, rushing from one room to the next, finding each empty but for a startled maid or footman. He cursed as he regretted the time he had wasted traveling to her father's townhouse. He hadn't been sure where to go first, and he had taken the chance that she had done as she said and visited him before leaving for the country. He could only hope that she hadn't told Woodward of her intentions, for it seemed the butler took his loyalties too far.

"Christina!" he called again, desperation in his voice as he bounded up the stairs two at a time. Finding her drawing room empty, he rushed down the hall to her bedchamber, pausing for but a moment when his eyes lit upon her and relief filled him.

Then his heart stopped as he saw the blood on her pale green dress, and for a moment, another memory came rushing back to him, the memory of Laura lying in a pool of her own blood. But now, the emotion that filled him was not the rage and injustice that had ruled him for so long, but a desperation that his own wife might suffer the same fate.

"Christina!" he repeated, more gently this time, and when she finally lifted her face to him, it was a sight he would never forget for the rest of his life. Her eyes were wide and staring, unfocused on anything, including him. She held her hands out in front of her, like Lady Macbeth in tableau.

"Daniel?" she said, her voice reedy thin, and he slowly moved toward her, noting Woodward lying on the floor. He didn't stop at the man, however, but rather moved to his wife, wrapping his arms around her and pulling her in tightly toward him. He knew he should loosen his grip, but he couldn't release her, so overcome he was with the fact that she was here, alive, apparently unhurt. The love he held for her washed over him, flooding through his body like rays of sun on a hot summer day. His relief quickly vanished, however, when he felt her trembling in his arms, and as much as he wanted to keep her tightly against him, he slowly pulled back to look at her.

He caught her chin between his thumb and forefinger and tilted her face toward him. "Christina, love, are you all right?"

She shook her head, a haunted look filling her gray eyes.

"I think I killed him," she said, her words but a whisper as she pointed at the floor. Daniel let go of her then, crouching down beside his butler. He noted the gash in the man's temple, but as he placed a hand on his chest, he felt the rise and fall of breath, and he turned to Christina, shaking his head.

"He's alive," he said.

"Oh!" She released a sigh of relief and sank to her knees beside him. "Thank God. Can you — can you get help for him?"

"Of course," he said. "But come, let us clean you up."

He began to lead her from the room, sensing she was still in somewhat of a daze when Lord Hudson arrived.

"Ravenhall— Good God!" he said, taking in the scene in front of him. "Are you all right, Lady Ravenhall?"

"Yes," she said, though her voice was still too strained for Daniel's liking. "I'm fine."

"Woodward needs medical attention," Daniel said to his friend, giving him an imploring look, which Hudson seemed to understand as he nodded back at him, and Daniel led Christina out through the door and into his own bedchamber. He knew he should call for her maid, but he found he did not want to leave her presence, preferring instead to see to her himself.

As she sat on his bed, the life seemed to come back into her face, for which he was vastly relieved. The color returned to her cheeks, and when she looked at him, her gaze was much sharper and focused.

"Christina," he said, smiling gently at her and picking up her hand. "I am so glad you are all right. After I confronted Lord Northcliffe, we ascertained what had happened — that Woodward had killed Laura, and might possibly be after you, were he to think you meant to do me any harm. Are you — are you truly all right?"

"I am, now that I know he's alive still," she said, her breath coming much more evenly now, though she sat back, away from him. "Thank you."

"What happened?" he asked softly.

"Apparently he set up a test for me. He sent a note making me believe you killed Northcliffe. I — I'm sorry, Daniel, but I decided I had to leave because of that, for the time being at least. Woodward felt that I was no longer good enough for you."

"It's all right. I think I understand now," he said, determined now to put all to rights. "You must know that I did not shoot Northcliffe. He is likely now being questioned as to his breaking into my home and threatening my wife. Woodward will be dealt with accordingly. But what matters most is that I have determined my ways of the past, some of the things I have done, that I meant to continue to do... they are over now, Christina. You have taught me what it means to be good, to be true to oneself, and I cannot thank you enough for that."

He stroked her cheek with the backs of his fingers, eliciting a tremor. "It is all over now, love," he finished, still looking into her eyes. "We have nothing to burden ourselves with any longer."

Christina looked back at him steadily as a single tear fell to her cheek.

"Is that so?" she asked with a sigh. "I am so very glad Daniel, that you didn't kill Lord Northcliffe, whether he was innocent or guilty. You are a better man than that, and I am happy you have come to see it for yourself. But Daniel — I have realized something. I cannot live like this. I *will* not live like this. I know you hold an affection for Laura still, and I understand you always will. I can share your heart with her. But I cannot be pushed to the side, treated with disdain, made love to, and then discarded."

He was stunned at her words. She had said she loved him. He thought they would move on, that all of this was behind them.

"B-but Christina," he stammered. "That is all finished with. I have put that part of my life behind me."

Daniel stared at his wife for a moment, taking in her tears and her agonized look, before dropping his gaze. She was right. Despite the fact that Laura had meant to marry another, he had cared for her, and he always would hold onto that with a piece of his heart. But he finally realized there was no need to feel any guilt over the love he now had for his wife. His memories would stay as just that — memories — while he found love anew.

"Do not run from me, Christina," he begged, grasping her hand as she stood. "I cannot allow this conversation — this *marriage* — to come to an end, not when there is so much that needs to be said, so much that needs to be explained."

She turned away from him, sitting down in a chair and putting her face in her hands.

"I cannot stay here, for the moment at least," she said with such stoicism, it nearly broke his heart. "I cannot be here, not when each day is an agony. I must live with the knowledge that the love I have for you will never be returned, and I cannot do that when I must be in your company every day of my life. It is too much." Tears began to fall from her eyes.

Daniel stared at her for a moment, his heart slowing down as he took in what she'd said. He did not know how to answer her, finding her revelation both astonishing and yet wondrous. Whether she'd meant to reveal it to him or not, she'd shown him her heart, and her heart was filled with love for him. A love he did not deserve and had not been able to speak aloud — not until today.

Carefully, Daniel knelt in front of his wife, cradling her hands in his and refusing to move, not even when she flinched at his touch. She had to know that he was here, had to know that he was not about to leave her side until he'd told her all he had to say.

CHAPTER 24

"Christina," he said, slowly. "My love for you has been growing steadily in the depths of my heart and I have simply refused to allow myself to see it. I hid it away, drowned it as best I could and yet still, it remained."

She said nothing, simply stared blankly at the *fleur-de-lis* pattern on the wall across from her.

"I must tell you the truth, love, and I pray that you will listen, for every word is spoken from my heart," he continued, gently. "Today, I stood in a quiet room with Northcliffe before me, my pistol aimed at his chest — and I could not take the shot. All I could think of was you. My mind and my heart were filled with you. I thought of your voice, your smile, your tenderness, and compassion. I thought of what our future could be like together, what I was about to throw away by taking vengeance in my own way. I finally chose to ignore my own desires and think only about you." He smiled gently as she turned her gaze back toward him.

"In that moment, I realized that I can have justice for Laura, but that I do not need to carry the guilt with me any longer. I am able to care for another without bringing any shame to my soul."

The only sound she made was a soft sniff.

"My past remains a memory — but it does remain in the past, just as it should," Daniel continued, reaching out to take hold of one of her hands. "In fact, I think, now that I know love with you, what I felt for her was affection, to be sure, but that was all it had time to develop into. I did not know her as I know you. I let anger take hold of me, and I allowed it to consume me. I became so determined to find justice for her death that it took hold of every part of my being. I refused to allow myself to feel, to love, to move on with my life. I was scared that if I gave you my heart, I would be betraying Laura's memory, but I realize now that it was not so."

"Christina," he whispered, knowing in his heart that he had to tell her the truth. "I have hidden this from myself and from you, but no longer." Looking up at her, Daniel felt his heart swell, his mouth curving into a gentle, beautiful smile. "Christina, I love you," he said, frankly.

Her eyes widened as she stared at him.

"I know I have been distant and cold, trying to keep away from you, but that was a ridiculous attempt to prevent the affection I felt growing into anything more." His smile grew. "As I think you can guess, that did not work particularly well."

Seeing the stains of tears on her cheeks, Daniel brushed them away with his thumbs.

"Christina," he whispered, as a slight blush touched her cheeks. "I have pretended I feel nothing when the truth is, I am amazed at how much my love for you continues to grow. Now that I have been able to see justice done, I feel as though my heart has been freed from its shackles and burst into life, sending a swell of love pouring through my veins. But that is because of you. It cannot be denied. It will not be denied. Oh, Christina, I will love you more with every day we spend together, if only you will give me another chance to prove myself to you."

Christina blinked, tears forming on her lashes again although they did not fall.

"Prove yourself?" she asked, softly, her hands warming under his own. "What do you mean, Daniel?"

He smiled at her, lifting one hand to brush his fingers down her cheek. "You told me that I was not the man who went out in a murderous rage, and you were right. But, at the time, I ignored your words, I did not heed your advice. I want to prove to you that I will listen to you, that I will respect you and that, most of all, I will love you with all that I have. You will not need to fear our future, for it will be one in which affection and trust abounds. I want to prove that I am not the distant, cold husband you have known, but that I can change into the husband you deserve."

His throat ached with a sudden sharp pain as he looked at his wife's face and took in her loveliness, almost overwhelmed by the depths in her eyes.

"I don't know, Daniel," she said, her words nearly breaking his heart. "I gave you my love willingly, without condition, and yet you seemed determined to push me away. I know you had demons — we all do — but I just wish that you had seen fit to trust me with your burdens, to share your life with me and allow me to be there with you. If something else threatens you or angers you, how do I know you will not shut me away again? And will you continue on this path of justice for others?"

"I understand what you feel," he said with a sigh. "Sometimes with all that I see in the world, it is difficult to have hope that all is not in darkness. I realize that. And I know, from the women I have helped, that it can be difficult to find that light again when it has been dark for so long. I promise that going forward, I will turn my focus solely on bettering lives of those who need it, and not on a quest for revenge." He paused, a thought coming to him. "Can I show you something? We will have to go for a carriage ride — but only if you feel well enough."

She hesitated but nodded. Daniel returned to her room, relieved to see Hudson had already removed Woodward, hopefully to find a physician. With little effort, he found what he knew to be her favorite day dress in the armoire and brought it to her. He untied the back of her gown, slipping it off her shoulders, marveling anew at her form.

As he helped her into the pale blue dress, she looked up at him, some wonder in her gaze. "How did you know—"

"That you would want this dress?" he finished. "I've seen how often you wear it, especially when you are reading or taking time to yourself. It is rather soft fabric, as well, and I thought something comfortable would be a good choice. Come now," he said, leading her to the hallway and down the stairs, halting at the bottom as he realized he had no butler to inform the stable master that he needed the carriage readied.

He led her out to the stables himself, surprising the young lads when he told them to ready the carriage. As he led her up to the seat, not wanting to let go, he could only hope that what she would see would change her opinion of him.

* * *

CHRISTINA TRIED to keep the frown from her face as she looked at her husband out of the corner of her eye. What could he possibly show her that would make any difference in determining what he felt for her, how he would treat her in the future? There was no way to determine that but time, she mused, and she couldn't torture herself by continuing to grow deeper in love with him if he was only to turn her away at the end of it all.

She was surprised when they traveled out of Mayfair, toward the poorer part of London, but they stopped just on the outskirts of St. Giles.

Daniel reached up a hand to help her down, and she certainly couldn't fault his attentiveness, as he tucked her hand in the crook of his arm, as if not wanting her too far away from him. They walked up to a nondescript house, though Christina realized it was fairly well taken care of in comparison to some of the other buildings around them.

"In here," he said, knocking on the door, and a slot was opened, only for two eyes to peer out at them.

"It is only me, Mrs. Smith," he said, and the door was opened, welcoming him in.

"Hello," Daniel said warmly. "May I present my wife, Lady Ravenhall? I thought she might enjoy a tour of the home."

Christina nodded at the woman, though she had a great number of questions as to where they were and what they were doing here.

"Oh, Lady Ravenhall," Mrs. Smith said. "How lovely to meet you. You are fortunate to have married a very, very generous man. Would you like to walk around, to meet some of the women?"

Christina realized then where they were — this was one of the houses Lord Hudson had told her about, where Daniel was helping women in need. She looked back at him, but he simply smiled at her and gave a wave of his hand.

"Go on," he said. "I will have to remain here, as men don't go beyond the entryway — even Lord Hudson and myself — for various reasons. But you are more than welcome to continue on."

Christina nodded and followed Mrs. Smith, very curious indeed.

CHAPTER 25

*D*aniel wrung his hands together as he waited for Christina. He didn't know if bringing her here would change anything, but he had to help her understand what he had seen, what haunted him so, why he had been so reluctant to allow her to see the feelings he held for her. He thought — he hoped — that bringing her here would help explain some of that, and that speaking to some of the women here would show her the possibilities of a second chance — for both of them.

When she finally returned, he jumped to his feet, but she wore a fairly indiscriminate expression.

"Thank you for your visit, Lord Ravenhall, Lady Ravenhall," Mrs. Smith said profusely. "We look forward to your return."

"Absolutely, Mrs. Smith," he said. "And thank you for your continued kindness."

Christina said nothing as they walked to the carriage, and when he sat beside her, he felt his heart pounding hard against his chest. Never before in his life — not even when he had approached Lord Northcliffe's room in the inn — had he felt such anticipation, knowing his life could change by the next words she uttered.

When she finally turned to him, however, her eyes were bright with a mixture of happiness and tears — and Daniel sighed with relief.

"I'm sorry I doubted you," she said, and he closed his eyes at her words. "Those women — those children — their lives have been saved because of you. You are a hero to them. I can only imagine what you have seen as you have helped people like them to find hope." She was quiet for a moment. "You are a good man, Daniel. I should have realized that, should have let your words be enough."

He shook his head. "I didn't give you any reason to trust me, any reason to come to know me at all as I forced the distance between us. Will you forgive me?"

"Of course I will," she whispered, leaning forward to look a little more keenly into his eyes. "I spoke to many of the women while I was inside. While some remain lost, scared, and hopeless, there are others who seem to be genuinely happy. Despite all they've gone through, how they've been treated, and what they have seen, they have hope for a better future, for themselves and for their children. They have that hope because of you. As with anyone, there is both darkness and light within you, but I think Daniel, that the light is beginning to win."

She paused for a moment.

"You came back to me, Daniel. You did not follow through with murder. You made a promise to me and kept it. You do wonderful, amazing things for those who need it. I want to share that life with you, as true husband and wife, to help you, to be there with you, by your side."

His throat worked, his hands tightening on hers as gratefulness overwhelmed him. Surely, he did not deserve her love, did not deserve to even have Christina as his wife.

"Your father should never once have told you that your beauty was nothing to speak of," he murmured, overcome as he framed her face with his hands. "You have more beauty than anyone I have ever met. You practically shine with your loveliness, your gentleness, and your kind heart. What I have done to deserve such an angel as you is quite beyond my understanding."

Her expression softened all the more as she lifted her arms around his neck and, resting her forehead against his, lingered there in silence. Daniel closed his eyes, choosing to simply be in the moment when all was finally at peace. The past was gone and all there was now was Christina.

"I love you, Daniel," Christina whispered, lifting her head just a little to look into his eyes. "I love you more than I can ever say."

He smiled at her then, amazed at how their difficult circumstances had somehow brought them together. "And I love you, Christina," he replied, one hand beginning to pull the pins from her hair, as a desperate urge to have her tresses running through his fingers tugged at him. "I will never leave your side — or your bed — again."

She laughed, her lips fleetingly brushing his before, finally, Daniel kissed her. It was soft and tender, a mending of two broken hearts, before the fire that began to burn inside of him grew ever hotter. Christina pulled away, her breathing ragged and heat burning in her gaze.

"I will never leave you again," Daniel repeated, lifting her so that she sat on his lap. "Let me prove it to you now."

"Daniel!" Christina giggled. "We are in a carriage in the middle of London!"

"I will have you fully attired by the time we reach home," he promised and was grateful when she nodded and laughed in agreement.

* * *

SHE HAD NEVER THOUGHT it possible to be as truly happy as she was in this moment. Christina's heart felt so full it was near bursting as she brought her palms around her husband's face, feeling the scratch of the stubble upon his chin.

While they had been married for near two months, it was only now, in this moment, that she finally understood what it meant to be a wife, to have a husband who returned all of the love and affection she felt for him in equal measure. It was beyond words, the emotion pouring through her soul, beginning in her chest and emanating outward to every part of her.

His laughter died as the crystal blue of his eyes roamed over her face.

"You are so very beautiful -- outwardly and within," he said, before gently kissing her lips. She fully expected him to ravage her mouth, but instead, he leaned back slightly and nibbled, creating a sensation that sent a shot of heat straight to her core.

Their love was something she had yearned for her entire life, but this — this passion was something she had never known was possible, a gift that she would have never known to ask for.

His strong hands came around her, one hand stroking the back of her neck, tilting her head to the side while his lips kissed a trail down her sensitive skin. His other hand came to her back, undoing the top few pearl buttons of her gown, the light touch of his fingers upon her skin causing her to shiver. He pulled her closer as he inched the shoulders of her dress down one side and then the other, his lips following where he removed the fabric.

"My God, I cannot get enough of you," he said, his voice ragged, and a surge of power blasted through her, that she was causing this feeling within him, this strength and weakness all in the same breath.

She brought her fingers to his cravat, clumsily undoing it, desperate to feel more of him. He took pity on her, helping her to loosen it before tossing it on the seat beside him. Daniel seemed much more interested in divesting her of her clothing, however, and he lowered her dress so that it sat under her bosom. He wasted no time in taking her breasts in his hands before bringing his mouth to the raised bud of one nipple.

She threw her head back at the majestic feel of his kisses, finally no longer ashamed of the size of her ample chest, as clearly, Daniel delighted in it. She could feel him hard against her, and she began to unlace the fall of his breeches, finding his thick manhood underneath. She stroked the smooth skin, and he jumped toward her, hastily lifting her skirts from around her legs so that she sat atop of him, flesh to flesh.

Christina couldn't keep herself from grinding against him, and he let out a pained groan before bringing his hand to her, stroking her for just a moment before he was apparently unable to wait any longer, and he lifted her up, making her gasp, before bringing her down on top of him. He filled her, making her feel utterly complete. Then his hands came to her hips, and he began to move her back and forth on top of him, until she found the motion herself and he let his hands fall away and return to her breasts, her hair, her back, seemingly everywhere at once as she rocked against him.

This time was different, in so many ways. She had the power to move as she pleased, to find what felt right to her. And this time, she was complete in the knowledge that her husband loved her with equal measure as she did him. This joining was not one to simply validate their marriage, but to celebrate what it meant.

The rush began to tingle throughout her body, and it

wasn't long before it burst into waves upon waves that flowed through her entire frame. She was still lost, languid in all the sensations when Daniel gave a shout and began to pulse within her, and she clutched him tightly to her while his release coursed through him.

They stayed like that, hanging onto one another, for what could have been seconds or minutes, she wasn't entirely certain. It seemed too soon that he murmured in her ear, "Time to dismount, love," before lifting her off of him and settling her beside him, and together they worked to redress themselves. Christina had just finished tucking the tendrils of hair back into her chignon when the carriage pulled to a stop, and she looked out the window at their townhouse.

"I told you I would have you back to a proper state by the time we arrived," Daniel said with a wicked grin. "And I will always follow through on my promises to you."

She smiled at him in return, trusting in all he said and knowing that he would be true to his word. He cocked his head and looked at her.

"How do you feel about the countryside?" he asked, and she tried not to show how much hope his words brought to her being.

"Oh, Daniel, I do enjoy it," she said in a rush. "Although, if you prefer to remain in London for a time, I understand. Wherever you need to be—"

"I would like nothing more than to take you to my country home if you're in agreement," he said. "I'm not one for the city, and while it now holds much better memories for me, I would like to show you what has felt much more like home for me over the years."

"That sounds wonderful," she said, clasping her hands together. "Although I shouldn't mind returning to London from time to time."

"Absolutely," he said, without any anguish or tenseness

filling his features. "This townhouse my parents forced upon me has rather grown on me, I must say."

"Like your bride?" she asked, quirking an eyebrow at him, causing him to laugh, a full, hearty chuckle unlike any she had ever heard from him. She hoped there would be much more in their future.

"My bride is another story altogether," he said, pulling her close once more. "I would say she has done more than grow on me. Rather, she has become part of me, a part that I could never bear to lose."

"Whatever may come, Daniel, our love is forever," she said, bringing her forehead to his.

"Forever," he repeated. "I promise."

EPILOGUE

*T*he happy music of laughter, voices, and babies cooing echoed around the drawing room of the country home, bouncing off the walls that at one point had seemed so empty and bleak. Not any longer.

Marie Harrington, Duchess of Ware, sat back in the corner of the chaise lounge as she looked around the room, her heart full. She didn't think she could ever have asked for more in her life or for the lives of her children. Oh, she knew the scene in front of her wouldn't be welcomed in the homes of many women of her station, and many in society would be scandalized by the way her family displayed their emotions. But that was not what Marie cared about. No, Marie's life goals were somewhat different than that of many like her. She simply wanted her children to be happy. Did that mean that she had given some of them a little push to find the one they were destined to be with? Perhaps. But, most of all, she and her husband simply hadn't stood in the way when they found the one they loved, whether or not their partners would have been the most acceptable for the son or daughter of a duke.

"You are making me nervous, Mother," Daniel, said as he walked toward her, a glass of port in hand. "I know that look."

"I do not know what you are talking about," she said, holding her nose in the air to let her son know that she didn't appreciate his remark, though inwardly she laughed at how transparent she had apparently become. Her children had grown too old, too wise. It made her sad for a moment as she longed for the carefree days of their youth, but in the same breath, she saw how much love they now had in their lives, and it brought a smile to her face.

"I am simply happy for you, Daniel," she said, holding out a hand to him and motioning to the seat beside her. He sat down with a smile and a warm look in his blue eyes, so like her own and that of the rest of her children. "I worried about you, you know. More than the rest."

He gave a low chuckle. "There were times in my life I wasn't sure I would ever feel joy again," he said with a shake of his head. "When you and Father threatened me into marriage, my God, did I resent you for it. But it seems you knew best after all."

She gave a very un-Duchess-like snort. "Of course I know best," she said. "If there is anything you should know, Daniel, it is that."

"And what will you do with yourself now that you no longer have marriages to arrange?" he asked, raising an eyebrow at her.

"Why, enjoy my grandchildren," she said, and then smiled when she saw Daniel's reaction to the words. He looked across the room at Christina, who was speaking with Benjamin's wife Sophie. As if sensing her husband's stare,

Christina looked at him, and they shared a small, secret smile that excited Marie in equal measure. Another grandchild, she thought, her heart swelling within her chest as she looked around the room.

There was a nursery in their lavish country home, of course, but she enjoyed having the children about, as did her husband. Thomas and Eleanor's girls, with their tanned skin and sun-kissed hair, were rather unruly, but they displayed their love with such openness it was hard to stay angry at them, even when they found continuous trouble. Even Eleanor had grown on Marie. She had been worried when Thomas married a woman who had lived most of her life away from England, but Eleanor loved their family and always ensured they spent ample time with them, which Marie appreciated.

Thomas came over to stand next to them, clinking a glass with his brother. They were all together to celebrate their parents' anniversary, though Marie thought it was rather foolish, as her husband barely remembered his own birthday let alone the day they were married or how many years it had been. Though, privately, she and Lionel had enjoyed reminiscing — not that they would share their own love story with their children. How they would be scandalized by their parents! Nevertheless, she was pleased to have any occasion for them all to gather.

Violet joined them, sitting next to her elder brother, her legs crossed at the ankles, her dark hair in a low, simple chignon as always. She smiled at her mother and Marie reached out a hand to clasp hers. How alike she and her daughter were — not just in looks, but in countenance. It was why they had never gotten along particularly well. Violet had her own mind and a determination to achieve all she had set out for.

"You look very well, Mother," Violet said, her hands

around the small bump that was just beginning to form, their second child.

"And you, darling," she said. "Greville and Taylor seem to be having quite the time of it over there."

"They always do," Violet said with a laugh. "How fortunate they ended up family, for Taylor would have been part of my life regardless."

"That's very true," her sister said, coming to stand next to Thomas. Now that Polly was older, they looked nearer to twins, Marie thought, and she was proud of the life Polly had made for herself. Marie still thought of Polly, her youngest, as a child in some ways, but the girl was now a mother herself, to a daughter who not only looked exactly like her but already at two seemed to have her temperament. Good, thought Marie. She will know exactly what it is like to raise a precocious child.

She swept her gaze to Benjamin. Ah, but how he had matured. To think that at one point he had been one of London's most well-known rogues, and now here he was, the doting husband of one of the gentlest, kindest women Marie had ever met.

Seeing them together, he came over and joined them, flashing his well-known, charming grin at his mother.

"This is quite the family reunion," he said. "Is there something of note?"

"Not at all," Marie said. "Simply that I am so proud of you all."

She felt tears begin to burn at the back of her eyes, and she tried her best to blink them away, knowing her children hated when she showed such emotion.

"It's all right, Mother," said Daniel, placing a hand on hers, and the touch of her eldest son, the one who at one point had been so afraid to show any emotion but anger and vengeance, made the tears start to fall. She looked over at her husband, who sat across the room with his dog at his feet, a drink in his hand, and his usual smile on his lips.

He nodded at her, knowing she would understand just all he was saying with the small gesture. Theirs had been a marriage meant to unite the power of two families. It had taken some time, but it had turned into so much more than that. They had developed a love that was lasting a lifetime and had ensured their children had found that same love in their own lives.

Now her children were gazing at her expectantly, and she felt the need to say something, to put into words all she felt inside.

"Love is a journey," she said simply. "A quest, if you will, to find one who can make life into more than simply an endless pattern of one day after another, but rather days full of honor, affection, trust, romance, and," she looked at Daniel, "Redemption. I cannot tell you how happy I am that you have all found that for yourselves. Your hearts are searching no longer but have found all that you wished for. For that, I am truly grateful."

As she finished speaking, a peal of laughter came from the corner of the room where the children played, and the tender moment was broken, but it was replaced by something just as wonderful, perhaps even better — the joy that came from a family that truly loved one another. And this love, well, this was what life was all about.

THE END

* * *

Dear reader,

I hope you enjoyed reading Daniel and Christina's story! If

you have read through the entire Searching Hearts series, then you will know that we have come to the end. I hope you enjoyed the Harrington siblings' searches for love. If you are interested in reading more of the family and haven't yet read it, you can find Marie and Lionel's story in a prequel, Duke of Christmas.

If you're looking for another series, The Bluestocking Scandals also features strong, independent women and men who love them. You can preview the first book in the series in the next few pages, or download it here: Designs on the Duke.

If you haven't yet signed up for my newsletter, I would love to have you join us! You will receive Unmasking a Duke for free, as well as links to giveaways, sales, new releases, and stories about my coffee addiction, my struggle to keep my plants alive, and how much trouble one loveable wolf-lookalike dog can get into.

www.elliestclair.com/ellies-newsletter

Or you can join my Facebook group, Ellie St. Clair's Ever Afters, and stay in touch daily.

Until next time, happy reading!

* * *

Designs on a Duke
The Bluestocking Scandals Book One

* * *

HER SECRET WILL SAVE A LEGACY. But it could also break her heart when faced with a duke caught between two identities.

The daughter of a famed architect, Rebecca Lambert has been raised among the nobility yet understands the circumstances of her birth. Becoming an architect is a dream, not an option, until she must assume an identity to protect her father's name.

No one was pleased when Valentine St. Vincent was shockingly named the Duke of Wyndham -- least of all Valentine himself. He has always led with his fists, but now he must become the man his brother was supposed to be.

When Valentine hires Rebecca's father, she takes on the work herself. But as she spends more and more time at the duke's homes, she finds herself hopelessly falling for a man she can never have. For the Duke of Wyndham must marry a woman for her dowry and respectability -- two things Rebecca can never provide.

Will Rebecca and Val resign themselves to the lives chosen for them, or those they were born to live?

AN EXCERPT FROM DESIGNS ON A DUKE

*T*he door knocker appeared to be frowning.

Rebecca tilted her head to better study the gigantic lion that stared her in the eye. This one was quite stoic and serious, its eyebrows narrowed in anger and, perhaps, a bit of worry. If the duke was attempting to discourage visitors, then he was certainly achieving his purpose.

"A door knocker should be welcoming, should it not?" she asked her father, who was making his own study of the front exterior of the house.

"It's a shame, really," he murmured, looking around. "A house of this size, in the middle of London, kept secret from all eyes for years now. Look at the gardens on the southern side! But Becca, this house... why it's not finished!"

"You're right," she said, her eyes widening. From afar it looked rather extravagant, but upon closer examination, all of the finishing details had not yet been completed. "We shall see what the interior holds. But Father, let's not tell him any of our thoughts on his home until we further determine just why he has asked us here."

"He quite obviously wants to hire us!" her father exclaimed indignantly. "I am in high demand, Becca. High demand! I have heard much of Wyndham House, you know. There were plans for it to be rather grand, but there is no need to determine just why it wasn't completed, for it is quite obvious. Clearly the initial design was flawed. The duke must know that I will *not* simply follow another's designs."

"Father, we need this commission," Rebecca said, tapping her foot nervously, hoping that her father would move on from his passionate criticism of what could be one of the grandest mansions in London.

All knew of Wyndham House, as it covered one of the largest footprints of any home in the city. But its fame was partially hinged on the fact that it had become something of a mystery.

It was nearly a decade now since the first brick had been laid, but for the past eight years, no one besides servants had set foot in it. The recently passed duke had been quite ill during his final years, and his visitors consisted solely of caretakers as he had no immediate relatives.

Which was partially why the dukedom had passed into the hands of this man, a far-removed cousin, who apparently had been unaware that he would someday become one of the most powerful men in England.

It was all quite intriguing. But Rebecca was intent on dismissing all of the gossip and fascination that surrounded the new duke and focusing on the task at hand. It would take all of her concentration to do so.

She took a deep breath as the door swung open.

"Good morning," said the man Rebecca assumed to be the

butler, though he was much younger than any butler she had ever met.

He was tall, handsome in a boyish way, and had a spark in his eye as he looked Rebecca up and down before turning his gaze onto her father.

"You must be Mr. Lambert," he said. "I am Dexter. Do come in."

Rebecca and her father stepped into the foyer, both of them immediately more interested in their surroundings than any of the human inhabitants.

The foyer was designed to impress but was lacking the details of a completed room. A dome in the ceiling had yet to be ornamented, and Rebecca thought that a gold inlay would make it sparkle like the sun. Perhaps with diamonds. There were cutouts in the wall for statues, the arched doorway beyond providing a glimpse of a grand staircase. How much better would it look, Rebecca mused, to be rid of the wall and have the staircase greet the arrivals? Something worth a discussion.

When they had finally finished their initial review as Dexter waited patiently, the three of them stood staring at one another.

"Is, ah, the duke in residence?" Rebecca finally asked. The butler, who stood before them, was unexpectedly hesitant.

"That's just the thing, Miss..."

"Lambert. Mr. Lambert is my father."

"Ah, yes, Miss Lambert. The duke was supposed to be here to meet you, but has not yet returned home."

"I see," Rebecca said, though, in truth, she was rather annoyed. So the new duke, despite his supposedly common upbringing, had already become like the rest of the nobility. "Shall we wait?"

"Of course," he said, though he made no move to show them into the house.

"Is the drawing room available?" she suggested with a raised eyebrow.

The butler looked rather flustered.

"Perhaps the parlor would be better."

"Very well," Rebecca said, willing patience.

So they were to be relegated to the parlor. Apparently they were not fine enough quality to be shown to the drawing room.

It was likely under the duke's own instructions. Rebecca had been around more than her fair share of the nobility as she had spent her life following her father from one commission to another. In some homes they were seen as upper servants, though her father had gained much respect over the years, the better his name became known. *She* was most often looked right through, seen almost like furniture.

"You see, Becca?" she heard her father murmur in her ear. "Unfinished. Ragged. Shameful."

He was right on the first two accounts. Despite the fact the house had been standing for a decade, many of the walls were bare, unadorned, some of the ceilings half-painted. Draperies covered some windows but not others, and furniture that had been accumulated had the look of that which was to have bided time until new furniture was procured.

That day had obviously not yet come.

They passed through the foyer and then into a long chamber that Rebecca guessed was to be a ballroom. It was currently empty except for two long tables, upon which sat a curious collection of objects.

She was so busy looking at their contents that she walked right into her father, who had stopped to stare at everything in front of him.

"What in the..."

"Father," Rebecca warned, cutting him off. Just then a jar

of green liquid on the table began to bubble, and Rebecca took a step backward, pulling her father with her.

Just as it exploded with white foam shooting out the top of the jar, a tall, slim woman dressed in green raced into the room.

"I'm so sorry," she said, clearly flustered as she attempted to push back some of the strands of blonde hair that floated around her face, though she refrained from touching her skin with her gloved hands. "I didn't know we were having company and I should have had this in another room. That being said, I think I am close to—"

"Jemima!"

"Oh, Mother!" the woman whirled around as an elegantly dressed white-haired woman *sailed* into the room — Rebecca didn't think walked was an adequate description. A strong floral scent wafted around her like a cloud.

"Hello there," she said, waving a hand in front of her demurely, giving Rebecca the idea that the woman hailed herself near to royal status — which, Rebecca supposed, she now was, as the immediate family of a duke. "You must be the architect. Please, do wait in the parlor. We look forward to our discussion. Dexter, please show them in. And next time, perhaps walk them the other way, through the drawing room?"

"Very well, Mrs. St. Vincent," he said with the slightest of bows and he waved a hand in the air, bidding them to continue to follow him.

Rebecca and her father exchanged a look, but Rebecca shrugged and urged her father to continue, though they both jumped at the bang that exploded from the table behind them.

"Sorry," the younger woman — Miss St. Vincent— said with a cringe and a bit of a wave before she returned to her work.

"How very curious," Rebecca's father murmured as they finally entered the parlor.

While this room, too, was not yet complete, Rebecca was drawn to the large Venetian window on the far wall, which overlooked the back court. A huge green expanse flourished beyond, though there was much potential to expand the gardens. This should be the focal point of the room, Rebecca thought. The furniture should look out beyond the window, the remainder of the room simple and unornamented.

The door opened behind them, and Rebecca turned, hoping to see the duke so they could be on with it, but instead it was the woman she assumed to be his mother.

"Wonderful to meet you, Mr. Lambert," she said with a wide, practiced smile on her face, as though they had not just encountered one another in the ballroom. She took a seat in one of the mismatched chairs, this one a royal-blue upholstered mahogany one that had been home to many bottoms, artfully arranging her expansive, clearly expensive, skirts over the chair so they fanned out evenly. "I am Mrs. St. Vincent and my son is the Duke of Wyndham."

"A pleasure to meet you," Rebecca's father said, his practiced charm emerging as he bent to kiss the woman's hand, though she pulled it away before he was able to do so.

"Yes, well. My son was supposed to be here to meet you, but unfortunately, he was called away on very *urgent* matters. As you may know, we have only recently arrived at this home in London, and as you can see, there is much to complete. I know my son has more particulars in mind and will review them once he arrives, but obviously the house has the potential to be *quite* opulent."

"Actually, Mrs. St. Vincent, we haven't seen much of it," Rebecca said, growing rather impatient. They hadn't much time to waste waiting. "Perhaps while we wait, we could tour the house?"

"And you are…?" she asked, fixing her pointed stare on Rebecca.

"Miss Lambert. I assist my father as his secretary."

"Oh. How unusual. Well. I suppose Dexter can show you around, if you must see it now."

They rose and Rebecca followed her father out. He began chattering away in Dexter's ear, and Rebecca followed behind, pulling out her sketchbook and making notes as well as drawing sketches and designs as she went.

The style was Palladian with a hint of neoclassical, she realized as they wandered through, and she wished she was able to better question the duke as to what had happened over the past decade. At least the current duke was willing to pay for additional work. While her father may have blamed shoddy design, the truth was evident. The previous duke had run out of money.

She poked her head into one room and then the other. It was a travesty, really, and Rebecca wondered what the country estate looked like. Stripped of all its finery, perhaps, in order to attempt to pay to keep up appearances? No wonder this place remained a mystery.

She stopped for a moment, attempting a quick drawing, when suddenly she realized how quiet the hall had become. Rebecca looked up to find that her father and Dexter were nowhere in sight. Drat. She had become too caught up.

She quickly ascended the staircase in an attempt to catch them, but the upstairs corridor was empty as well. Rebecca put her ear against one door and then the next, but there was no sign of them. There was, however, a door slightly ajar at the end of the hall. She continued toward it, pushing it fully open to reveal a long, wide bedchamber. The windows were covered in heavy navy draperies, the bed itself taking up a large portion of the room. Goodness, how large was the duke that he needed such space?

Curious, Rebecca walked further into the room, though she was aware that this was likely not one of the rooms Dexter would have included in his tour. But she couldn't help herself. She loved studying how people lived. And, unlike many rooms in the house, this chamber was obviously occupied.

There was a small dressing room and another door that Rebecca assumed connected to another bedroom. She pushed it open, finding the bedroom entirely bare. So there was clearly no *her* grace. Rebecca was about to retreat when she heard a heavy tread in the hallway, the steps coming closer and finally entering the room.

Not the wandering, unhurried steps of her father. Not the quick steps of Dexter.

It must be the duke.

Her heart began to race at the thought of being caught in the bedchamber of one of the highest peers in all of England. How would she ever explain herself? Rebecca did the first thing that came into her mind.

She hid.

Keep reading Designs on a Duke here!

ALSO BY ELLIE ST. CLAIR

Blooming Brides

A Duke for Daisy

A Marquess for Marigold

An Earl for Iris

A Viscount for Violet

The Blooming Brides Box Set: Books 1-4

Happily Ever After

The Duke She Wished For

Someday Her Duke Will Come

Once Upon a Duke's Dream

He's a Duke, But I Love Him

Loved by the Viscount

Because the Earl Loved Me

Happily Ever After Box Set Books 1-3

Happily Ever After Box Set Books 4-6

The Victorian Highlanders

Duncan's Christmas - (prequel)

Callum's Vow

Finlay's Duty

Adam's Call

Roderick's Purpose

Peggy's Love

The Victorian Highlanders Box Set Books 1-5

Christmas

Christmastide with His Countess

Her Christmas Wish

Merry Misrule

A Match Made at Christmas

A Match Made in Winter

Standalones

Always Your Love

The Stormswept Stowaway

A Touch of Temptation

For a full list of all of Ellie's books, please see
www.elliestclair.com/books.

ABOUT THE AUTHOR

Ellie has always loved reading, writing, and history. For many years she has written short stories, non-fiction, and has worked on her true love and passion -- romance novels.

In every era there is the chance for romance, and Ellie enjoys exploring many different time periods, cultures, and geographic locations. No matter when or where, love can always prevail. She has a particular soft spot for the bad boys of history, and loves a strong heroine in her stories.

Ellie and her husband love nothing more than spending time at home with their two sons and Husky cross. Ellie can typically be found at the lake in the summer, pushing the stroller all year round, and, of course, with her computer in her lap or a book in hand.

She also loves corresponding with readers, so be sure to contact her!

www.elliestclair.com
ellie@elliestclair.com

Printed in Great Britain
by Amazon

48783635R00126